ANY WAY YOU LOOK

Also by Maleeha Siddiqui

Barakah Beats

Bhai for Now

MALEEHA SIDDIQUI

ANY WAY YOU LOOK

SCHOLASTIC PRESS
NEW YORK

All rights reserved. Published by Scholastic Press, an imprint of Scholastic Inc., *Publishers since 1920*. SCHOLASTIC, SCHOLASTIC PRESS, and associated logos are trademarks and/or registered trademarks of Scholastic Inc.

The publisher does not have any control over and does not assume any responsibility for author or third-party websites or their content.

Library of Congress Cataloging-in-Publication Data available

ISBN 978-1-339-01026-7

10 9 8 7 6 5 4 3 2 1   24 25 26 27 28

Printed in Italy   183

First edition, May 2024

Book design by Omou Barry

For my sisters: Nawal, Nida, Aiman, Suha, and Safa

MSNSAN(TA) forever <3

CHAPTER 1

I know that look on the pink-hijabed lady's face. She's falling in love, but she doesn't know it yet.

I've been spying on auntie here for the last fifteen minutes, pretending like I don't notice when her gaze first lands on the shimmering white-gold dress draping our mannequin, how she lightly touches the fabric and admires the fancy beadwork on the skirts. Even when she turns to browse other booths set up around the hotel's grand ballroom, she keeps stealing glances over at our dress like it's calling her name.

Come on, come on, I think, the tip of my tongue sticking out of one corner of my mouth hungrily as my eyes follow her around the room. *You know you want it. Can't resist forever, lady.*

But she moves on, drifting to the other side of the hall. The spell was probably broken by another seller dangling their shiny product in front of her face. It's the summer exhibition, after all. The biggest one of the year. Everyone's looking for a good deal. The turnout at these events is always amazing, which makes for free advertising and tons of exposure for small businesses like my mom's, so they're super important.

I'm manning our booth while my sister checks out the hall and Amma tracks down my little brother, Kashif. He bailed on us a while ago. He's probably playing with all the other nine-year-old kids forced to be here. Since no one else looks like they're going to come up to me for now, I kick my sandals up on the footstool underneath our table and go back to watching my favorite TikTok costume designer re-create another Disney Princess gown. She always adds her own little spin to it. The fabric she's working with is so stretchy and sparkly! I fantasize about making a desi princess dress with that material. Something that Sania Maskatiya or Farah Talib Aziz—two of my favorite Pakistani fashion designers— or Jasmine Fares, my modest fashion icon, would approve of. I've always been into the fancier stuff. Before I know it, my head fills with shapes, patterns, fabrics, and color combinations—burgundy and rose gold, baby blue and tea pink, cherry red and teal. I wish I were back home or in the shop. Whenever inspiration hits me like this, I need to be able to get all my ideas down, to sketch the dress swirling around in my head on Amma's tablet.

But instead, I'm here. I guess I should feel lucky Amma let me come to the exhibition at all, even though it's a Saturday and there's only one week of sixth grade left before summer break. School's a big deal for Amma, and she's not okay with me getting distracted until classes are done for real.

"How much for that one?"

I almost fall out of my chair in surprise, but I catch myself just in time. The pink-hijab lady—she's back! And what do you know, she's pointing at the white-gold dress displayed at the end of our table.

"It costs, uh—" Ack, I don't know! Heart racing, I search the crowded room for Amma and my older sister, Kulsoom, but they're nowhere in sight. *Stay calm, Ainy. Don't scare the customer away!*

Because even though I hate this part, making lots of sales is how Amma makes money. She can make a lot more in this one weekend than she can in a couple of weeks! And with Abu gone to Pakistan to help my dadi, who was diagnosed with cancer, Amma's business is our only source of income. And I can't talk Amma into letting me work for her this summer if the store shuts down, so . . .

I paste on my best smile for the woman. "That one?" I ask sweetly. "It's beautiful, right? One of a kind!"

The woman—she's South Asian, Pakistani like me, or maybe Bangladeshi—looks me up and down in my sparkling silver-and-turquoise shalwar kameez. I'm wearing matching earrings and a long necklace, tied together with some light mascara and a swipe of lip gloss. My short hair is pushed back with a thick headband, and it's showing off more of my face, which, over the last several months, has been losing its usual roundness and making my big, dark eyes pop. The lady's probably wondering if it'd be weird to haggle with a twelve-year-old. She better not start with me, because there's no way—

"Seven hundred," someone says. I breathe a sigh of relief. Kulsoom—I call her Bajjo—appears with her best friend, Amarah, in tow and sets down a bowl of chaat in her empty chair. My sister is all business in makeup and a light-blue blazer, her printed headscarf pinned expertly to drape across one shoulder in a style that I've tried to copy more than a hundred times but can never seem to get right. Bajjo's whole outfit is giving vibes of Melanie Elturk, the trendy CEO of the biggest hijab fashion brand in the world, Haute Hijab. Bajjo's the perfect straight A student, debate and Model UN member, active community volunteer, and all-around super girl. Plus, she's the greatest big sister in the world and my role model.

One day, I want to wear the hijab full-time like her, too. I've been taking baby steps, going to the masjid with her more often to test the waters since it's pretty much required to wear a hijab when we're there. If Bajjo can do it, I can do it. I just need to up my game to her level of awesome.

The pink-hijab auntie gasps at the price and puts a hand over her heart. "Dollars?!" she exclaims.

Bajjo wipes her mouth with a napkin before turning back to face the woman. "It's very fancy. Perfect for any formal event," Bajjo offers without missing a beat. I cheer her on inside.

"But that's still so expensive!"

"Actually, it's a bargain." Amma finally returns, her gold-trimmed abaya fluttering at her heels. Her voice is smooth behind her niqab. "That dress took over a hundred hours to make. Everything you see here is specially designed and handmade. Nothing's imported."

That's Amma's biggest selling point. Most of the other vendors here have their traditional clothes shipped to them from their home countries because there aren't a lot of options for desi clothes in the US. But Amma took advantage of the gap in the US market. Not everyone has family or knows someone overseas who can ship clothes to them at a moment's notice or has the time and money for such a lengthy process. So, Amma brought the convenience of shopping at Pakistani markets here. Amma's the only one in our community who does what she does. Custom designs for all occasions; tailoring; quality craftsmanship. After years of running the business from home, she finally opened her own storefront a few months ago. I know firsthand how much work it is because I've been falling asleep to the sounds of her sewing machine for as long as I can remember. So, auntie here can buzz off with her it's-so-expensive attitude. The same dress would cost ten times more from anywhere else. And I might be biased, but Amma's definitely got the best inventory in the house.

"*You* made all of these?" the woman asks, and you can't miss the disbelief coloring her words as she stares at Amma—more specifically, at her niqab. I grin. This lady should get a load of what Amma's wearing underneath her floor-length abaya right this minute. Amma dresses in the most beautiful abayas, hijabs, and niqabs whenever she goes out. At home, she wears real gold jewelry (what's left of her inheritance that she didn't use to open Naseerah's Almari, that is) and makeup. Amma is always underestimated by people for wearing the niqab—including other Muslims who thought Amma covering her face was "too extreme." It never gets old seeing how they go from treating her like she's talentless and drab just because she dresses very modestly in public to shock when they discover she actually has a sense of style.

Amma doesn't flinch, only nods and stares right back at the woman.

She tsks. "I can give you five hundred for the dress," she says, fishing for cash in her designer purse.

"Sorry, ma'am, I'm afraid we can't accept that," Bajjo says before Amma can respond. She sounds like a professional. Ever since Naseerah's Almari's grand opening, Bajjo's been spending a lot of time helping out. She's going to be a junior in the fall and has to prepare for the SATs and start thinking about college applications, but Amma's not worried about *her* grades slipping. Meanwhile, I have to beg for permission to even set foot inside the store. Apparently, aspiring to be best dressed everywhere I go isn't as impressive as being an academic overachiever.

"Oh no, surely you can do something—?" the lady presses on.

But Bajjo holds firm. "Seven hundred is more than a fair price for that dress, and we won't be taking another cent off. Thank you for your interest, though."

Realizing we aren't budging, the lady turns her nose up and stalks off.

"Cheapskate," Bajjo mutters under her breath when she's gone.

"I could've marked it down by another fifty or a hundred dollars for her . . ." Amma says uncertainly.

"For *that* dress?" Amarah squeals. "No way, Naseerah Auntie! You should be charging at least a thousand dollars for it. And we know most people here can afford it. They just act like they can't to save money."

Amma still looks sad that she lost a customer. I know how much it must hurt, but that auntie really was being unfair.

"Can I look around now?" I ask.

"Sure, Ainy. Thanks for keeping an eye on things,"

Amma says. "Go take a break. I saw Safiya and her mom earlier."

"We're coming, too," Bajjo says. "Amma, you good here?"

"Haan, beta," Amma says. "I think I can manage by myself. You girls have fun. Don't worry about Kashif. I found him eating with some friends in the conference center." She waves us off.

"Thanks for the save," I tell Bajjo as she, Amarah, and I skirt around our table and enter a maze of dozens of stalls and booths boasting everything from casual to chic shalwar kameez, party and bridal dresses, colorful lehengas, abayas, silky shawls, glittering chudiyan, and shoes—so much stuff it makes me dizzy.

"It was nothing," Bajjo replies. "You were already doing great."

"But you handled that auntie like a boss! Not that I'm surprised. You're good at everything," I say appreciatively.

Bajjo shrugs and grabs my sleeve to pull me along behind her and Amarah. She knows I'm tempted to stop and gawk at everything. I can't help it; I thirst after all the shiny things even though I can't afford most of it.

Amma says I was born loving fashion, just like her.

When I was four, I used to change my outfit three times a day and strut around the house. At six, I was already complaining about having nothing to wear to parties. When I turned eight, Amma taught me how to sew and bought me my first sewing machine kit. I've been obsessed with fashion ever since.

We elbow our way through the herd and into the much quieter, less chaotic lobby to take a breather. A couple of smaller kiosks are selling things like homemade accessories and cosmetics next to the indoor fountain.

While Bajjo and Amarah check out fancy hijabs, I text my best friend, Safiya, to ask where she is.

Safiya: we left, sorry!! :(noor was being fussy
Me: you around later?
Safiya: mama has a bride this afternoon and then we're going out for my aunt's birthday.

Safiya's mom is a beautician and runs a salon out of their basement. The Messaoudis are the kind of people who always have plans. Social to the max degree. But I guess that's normal when both sides of your ginormous family live nearby.

I'm upset that I missed her, though. Safiya's five-month-old baby sister, Noor, has taken over their lives. Her parents are always too busy or too tired to drop Safiya off to hang out with me outside of school as much anymore. It's been driving Safiya up the wall.

"Hey, Ainy." Amarah pokes my arm and I look up from my phone at the goofy smile on her face. "Izyaan was asking about you this morning. He wanted to know if you were going to be here."

"He did?" I ask. Amarah and Bajjo giggle at my reaction and my cheeks flame.

Izyaan is Amarah's little brother. We've known their family since forever. Izyaan and I have always been around each other since our big sisters are inseparable, so we became friends by default.

But something . . . changed . . . when middle school started. Izyaan was in my Language Arts class this year, so I saw him every day in addition to on the bus before and after school. At some point this past year I became fascinated by how he'd run his fingers through his black hair. How he slowly inched his way taller than me, how he started wearing

11

clothes that fit his frame better, how his white teeth flashed against his dark brown skin whenever we ran into each other between classes. One time we were all at a mutual family friend's dawat, and he tried handing me a glass of Fanta (orange soda hits, okay?). I spilled it all over us because I was too distracted by his face. Bajjo and Amarah had a field day. And now that we live in Amarah and Izyaan's basement, they have more reasons to make fun of me.

"You like him," Amarah coos.

"Ssshhh!" I hiss, horrified that the aunties next to us are going to hear them teasing me. Worse, I realize, they're two of Amma's friends—Aaira Auntie and Lubna Auntie. Their heads are pressed together as they compete to talk over each other furiously.

"Still unmarried," Aaira Auntie is saying exasperatedly in Urdu. "Not a single good match. There was one, and the guy was perfect. Handsome, comes from a good family, settled with a respectable job, but he has one condition: He doesn't want a hijabi."

Aaira Auntie shakes her head at the neatly folded scarves on sale like she's at a funeral. "Arey, boys nowadays are like that. Kiya kar sak tai hai?" *What can we do?* "Poor girl's parents are stressed. They even asked her to take her hijab off, at least until she's married, so she can attract good men while she can, but she won't listen. Absolutely refuses to take it off."

"Good for her," Bajjo mutters, but not quietly enough. Aaira Auntie catches sight of us over Lubna Auntie's shoulder and beams. "Oh, asalamualaikum! Kaisi ho, betiyan? Shopping kaise chal rahi hai?" *How are you, dears? How's the shopping going?*

Bajjo and Amarah mumble replies, but that instinct to respect my elders and be a better cheerleader for Amma makes me pipe up. "Good, Auntie! Amma's here, too. You should go check out our table inside. She's got some new pieces."

"Acha? Chalo, let's go see," Lubna Auntie says. "Naseerah always has just what I need." She ushers Aaira Auntie inside the bustling ballroom.

"Nice work, Ainy," says Amarah. "Oh, that one is pretty." She points at the ready-made maroon hijab with black lacework and glittering stars I picked up.

Bajjo frowns. "You sure you're ready for the hijab? Not everyone thinks like Lubna Auntie and Aaira Auntie, but trust me, that's not even half the crap you're gonna have to put up with."

I bunch up my eyebrows. This is the one topic my sister and I can never agree on. Bajjo could be more supportive and say *Don't listen to them, Ainy* instead of trying to talk me out of it. But that's all she's been doing ever since I told her I want to start wearing the hijab. *You're too little. You don't get it. It's not that easy.*

But I *want* to. And that's enough for me. I don't get why it isn't enough for her.

CHAPTER 2

It's field day, which means there are only two more days until sixth grade's over. No more Amma breathing down my neck every night until my homework's done. Two more days stand between me and freedom.

And by *freedom*, I mean the mile-long list of plans Safiya's making as she takes notes on her phone. Safiya's the only reason I have any kind of social life.

"So, we've got movie night and sleepovers most Fridays, followed by crepes for brunch," Safiya says. "We're gonna binge *Ms. Marvel* together. There's Family Day at the theme park, of course. How can we miss that? I'm taking that Women in Islam seminar with Sister Ambreen every Thursday, so you could join that if you want to. There's our monthly halaqah. My dad got a new grill, so he wants to do a lot of cookouts. Oh, and I've got a stack of books I need to catch up on. Do you wanna do a buddy read—?"

"Hey, whoa, slow down!" I laugh, slinging myself onto the grass. It's hot as an oven out here, making everyone's ugly matching field day T-shirts stick to their skin. Safiya and I found a shady spot close to the basketball court. A bunch of sixth graders are milling about, signing one another's yearbooks. The seventh and eighth graders are enjoying games and rides spread out on the soccer field. The older students kept calling dibs on stuff, so most of us sixth graders decided it's easier to stay out of their way.

"Do we get to, like, sleep in at all?" I ask. Even for Safiya, this is going way overboard. I'm pretty sure she's throwing out whatever comes to mind at this point. Except . . . "You forgot swimming."

"The pool!" Safiya slaps her forehead, making her earrings jingle. She always wears her hijab in a style that makes them peek out. Today, they're simple silver hoops with tiny bells at the ends. "I can't believe I forgot! Hang on, let me add that to the list."

Amma loves Safiya, but she never ceases to be amazed by Safiya's impressive inability to hold still.

"No trip this time?" I ask Safiya. She's Pakistani on her mom's side and Algerian on her dad's, and some years her family spends a few weeks in Pakistan and Algeria. She always brings me back gifts from both countries, usually jewelry and new cultural clothes. I wonder if Abu will do the same when he returns, after Dadi gets better. I've never met my grandmother—only talked to her over the occasional FaceTime call—but the thought of her being that sick makes my chest twinge with sadness, especially for Abu.

"Nope. Noor's too little." Safiya fidgets on the grass like it's prickling her legs and tosses her phone from one hand to the other. "But that means we get to spend the entire break together! I can't wait to get out of the house. I'm so sick of all the *crying*." Safiya breathes in through her nose and out through her mouth meditatively. "Just a few more days. So close, yet so far."

Tell me about it. I had to do summer school last year because I didn't pass my standardized tests and Amma freaked out thinking they wouldn't let me move up to middle school. Ever since, everything is *school school education blah blah blah*. Apparently, one mistake means I'm doomed to flunk out forever. That's why Amma never lets me help with her business. Not even with the small tasks, let alone designing.

But this summer's going to be different. I'm going to

level up on my fashion game. I'm going to get so good at designing clothes that Amma will want me to help her all the time.

"I'm going to ask my mom if I can work at the store," I tell Safiya.

Safiya straightens excitedly. "Really? Do you think she'll let you?"

"I worked my butt off in all my classes this year," I say. "She better."

"I hope she says yes, but if you get a job this summer, then that's going to cut into *our* time." Safiya makes a sad-puppy face. "You won't forget me if you're hired, right?"

"No way! Besides, I don't even know if Amma will agree, so just in case, prepare to be sick of me."

"Sick of *you*?" a familiar voice says from behind us. "Doubt it."

We turn our heads to find Izyaan and two other guys in our grade—Yasir and Mustafa—standing over us with their yearbooks.

"Oh. Hi," I stammer, blushing. Giddiness tickles my stomach when Izyaan smiles down at me with his sparkly white teeth. *It's just Izyaan. You've known him since you were five. Don't act like such a loser.* Beside me, Safiya is making quiet lovey-dovey noises. I resist the urge to smack her. I never used to melt like this around Izyaan before. It's like when middle school started, this bubbling attraction suddenly rose to the surface and now he's too cute for me to handle. Plus, Izyaan's literally one of the nicest guys you will ever meet. It's hard *not* to like him. Which makes it ten times harder for me to act casual when he's around.

"Can we help you?" Safiya asks them in a floaty voice edged with ice. Her mean tone is only directed at Yasir and Mustafa, but especially Mustafa. Safiya's had a personal grudge against him ever since she, Mustafa, and Rachel Moore were the only kids left in their social studies class without a partner for an in-class worksheet and Mustafa chose to work with Rachel instead of Safiya. Everyone knows Rachel's a total ditz, and Safiya's convinced Mustafa didn't want to work with her because they're both Muslim.

"I just wanna know who these brown boys think they are," Safiya vented to me at lunch that day. Her face was redder than a tomato. "What are they trying to prove? They're embarrassed of *us*? They think we're ugly? Please! Ninety percent of them don't even brush their teeth! I hope they all fall into a ditch! I hope they never hit puberty and stay sounding like squeaky mice forever!"

I laugh at the memory.

"What's so funny?" Izyaan asks.

I blush again. "Oh, nothing. Uh—I—was just—remembering something?"

"Ohhhkay," he says, smiling. "Will you guys sign my yearbook?"

"Sure," I croak, taking the yearbook and a blue pen from his outstretched hands. I flip to a page that doesn't have dozens of signatures crammed onto it. My hand shakes as I try to come up with what to write. *You're the best!* Too creepy. *Have a great summer!* Talk about unoriginal. My armpits start to sweat the longer I stall with Izyaan's yearbook open against my knees. In the end, I settle for *Language arts was a lot of fun! Thanks for always helping me study for the vocab quizzes! I hope we have classes together again next year! :)—Ainy.*

Wait, is that too many exclamation points?

Safiya clears her throat loudly. Jolted, I quickly pass Izyaan's yearbook to her.

Yasir steps forward and thrusts his yearbook at me. "Mine next," he says, like it's not up for debate. "And make sure you sign next to your photo."

"Yes, Your Highness," Safiya mutters, rolling her eyes. "Whatever you say."

I flip to my school picture. Mine's at the beginning of

the row, so it's easy to write in the white space. As I look at my photo, a realization hits me: This could be the last-ever school picture of me without a hijab. Next school year, if I finally take the leap, I'll walk through the doors of seventh grade as a full-time hijabi. I've been thinking about it for a while now, but for weeks a small pang has been growing in my heart whenever I look at Bajjo, Amarah, and Safiya. They all wear it and it makes me feel left out. Like I'm missing something, or I'm not trying hard enough to be a good Muslim. Safiya started this year and I've noticed she's really gotten into deen stuff ever since. I want to be like that, too. To be someone other girls can look up to. To look and *feel* close to my religion. Because no matter how hard I try, I can't shake the feeling that I'm falling behind everyone else in that department, and now I have to catch up to them.

I sign only my name and try handing his yearbook to Safiya next, but Yasir takes it from my hands. He peers at my signature with a frown, like he was expecting a bouquet of roses and got worms instead. I look at him curiously. When he notices me staring, a little half smile creeps across his face. I don't return it. Yasir's not bad in terms of his looks. He just has a yuck personality.

Mustafa doesn't ask me or Safiya to sign his yearbook. He just bumps Yasir's shoulder in some bro code fashion, wriggling his eyebrows at Yasir until Safiya returns Izyaan's yearbook to him.

"Thanks!" says Izyaan. "Why are you guys sitting here anyway? It's field day. Don't you wanna hang out on, you know, the field?"

Safiya throws her arm over her eyes dramatically. "It's too hot to even exist right now. But we won't complain if you want to bring us some lemonade. Mint, please."

"Sure. Strawberry for you, Ainy?"

My cheeks grow warmer. "No. I mean, yes. You don't have to—"

"I got 'em. Wait right here." Izyaan sets his yearbook down on the grass next to me and jogs over to the drinks stand with Yasir and Mustafa trailing a few feet behind him. I wonder if they know that we can see them whispering to each other behind Izyaan's back. Or that they keep casting sneaky glances over at us.

Safiya wrinkles her nose at Yasir and Mustafa. "I still don't get why Izyaan hangs out with them. They're the worst."

"Well, Yasir's his cousin," I say, like that explains everything.

"Who cares? Tell them to kick rocks. Izyaan can do so much better."

I flash an angelic grin. "Not better than me, right?"

"No chance. You're the real deal. Not even lover boy is at your level."

I cringe. "Ew, Safiya! Don't say that out loud!"

Izyaan returns with our lemonades, and he sits down with us to ask us what our plans are for the summer. Safiya opens her mouth, no doubt prepared to rattle off her list, but I hold up my hand and groan. "Don't ask," I say. "We'll be here all day."

CHAPTER 3

I get home from school and enter Amarah and Izyaan's basement through the backyard, kicking my shoes off on the patio under the structural awning supporting the Khalids' deck. I'm surprised to find Amma sitting at our dining table in front of her laptop. I thought for sure she was going to put in a little overtime after closing the store all weekend to take part in the exhibition. Looks like it was worth it, though, judging by the heaps of garment bags labeled with receipts dotting the floor around her.

"Asalamualaikum," Amma chimes when I step through the sliding glass door. "Sorry about the mess."

"What mess?" I say jokingly. There're always lengths of thread scattered all over the carpet, pieces of cut cloth strewn on the ugly white tile in the kitchen, empty spools and missing needles turning up in unexpected places. Wearing socks or slippers indoors is a must at this point.

I set my backpack down and head to the bathroom. I take a quick shower to wash off the gross feeling on my skin from the summer heat. Glad to finally be rid of my awful field day T-shirt, I dig out my favorite pair of pajamas from underneath the huge mess on my bed—tangled jewelry, hair clips, small fabric swatches I swiped from Amma's storage bin, my favorite fashion illustration book, markers, magazines. I might spend a lot of time carefully putting myself together when I go out, but at home I'm a slob.

Refreshed, I dig through the drawers of our tiny kitchen for a snack and plop down across from Amma. It's just the two of us. The high school lets out later so Bajjo's not home yet, and if I had to guess, Kashif's out shooting hoops with some of the other neighborhood kids.

"What's that?" I ask through a mouthful of Halal Crispy Treat, pointing at the scribble-filled notepad next to Amma's laptop.

"My never-ending to-do list." Amma sighs, blowing a strand of black hair out of her tired face. Out of my siblings and me, I look the most like her, but of course you wouldn't know that unless you saw Amma niqab-less. I just prefer Western clothes over Amma's colorful assortment of casual shalwar kameez. Most of which she sewed herself from leftover cloth that clients told her she could throw away. Let's just say they're not cheap.

"It was slow at the store today, so I thought I might knock a few things out," says Amma. "I didn't realize running this as a full-fledged business would involve so many hours *not* making clothes. Kulsoom ordered new business cards and updated the website last night, but there's still a million other things to do."

This is my chance. "Sounds like you could use more help," I suggest. I splay my arms out wide in an imitation of a starfish. "I volunteer!"

"You have school, Ainy."

"For, like, two more days!" I protest. "We're having end-of-the-year parties in all my classes. We're not learning anything useful. I haven't had homework in over a week. Check my dashboard." Amma has my password, so she can check to see if I'm lying about not having any assignments. Not that I ever lie in the first place. I don't hide things from Amma or Bajjo.

"I still don't think that would be a good use of your time," Amma says, leaning back in her chair. "You could enroll in summer classes to get ahead instead."

"Amma, no!" I whine, kicking my legs like a toddler.

"Stop that, Quratulain," Amma chides, catching the back of my flailing legs with her foot. "You are not a baby."

My full name is Quratulain. Yeah. Thanks for that, Abu. I've always gone by the short version: Ainy. It's way cuter, and *Ainy Zain* would make a killer brand name one day—*if* Amma would give me lessons, like back in the old days when she wasn't so busy.

"I want to help you at Naseerah's Almari. You can't use my grades as an excuse anymore. I even made the honor roll." I practically sprawl across her lap with my hands folded in front of her face. "Please, please, please. I'll be the best employee ever. I'll bring you chai whenever you want. I'll clean up every day. You don't even have to pay me—"

Amma laughs. "You made your point. You did do very well in school this year, and I'm proud of you for working hard." Amma considers the ceiling resignedly. "Well, Kulsoom won't be able to help as much this summer because she got another part-time job. And it would take a lot of time and effort to find another full-time employee . . . But then what am I going to do about Kashif? He can't stay home alone all day."

Amma draws her gaze from her laptop screen to her notepad to the orders piled up around the basement. There are only two bedrooms—one for Amma, and one for Bajjo and me that you have to walk through the kitchen to reach—plus one full bathroom that we all share. Kashif sleeps on the pull-out couch. All our furniture is used or secondhand. We've been struggling ever since my aunt and uncle brought us to the US, and then they ditched us to move to Texas. Basically, they were like *Welcome to America! Good luck!* and peaced out. Bajjo was only four at the time and I was "due in five minutes." Amma and Abu have never forgotten how our family abandoned us. Abu didn't get a very good education back in Pakistan, so he worked cashier jobs before finding a position as a residential security guard. And then three months ago he had to give that up to take care of my grandmother overseas. He didn't want to leave us, but Amma made him go. Without him, we couldn't afford to keep living in our apartment. Luckily, Amarah and Izyaan's parents offered to let us rent their basement, so here we are.

I've never asked for anything that I know my parents

can't give me, but working at the store is something Amma *can* let me have.

Amma lets out a breath, and I hold very still in anticipation. "Okay," she finally relents. "Let me check to see if Sister Ambreen is okay with looking after Kashif, and then you can come to the store with me. But *just* for the summer. After that—"

She doesn't get to finish her sentence because my Crispy Treat flies out of my hand and I'm tackling her in a bear hug. "Thank you, thank you!" I exclaim. "I can't wait! This is going to be the best summer ever!"

"Don't get too excited now," Amma says with fake sternness. "I expect you to pull your weight, young lady."

"Teach me everything," I say.

"In shaa Allah," says Amma. "For now, can you find Kashif and tell him it's time to come back inside? I gave him one hour and it's been longer than that."

Ugh, this is why my little brother needs a phone. But since Amma looks spent and she probably doesn't want to put on her abaya and niqab just to track him down, I agree.

The first place I check is up and down the street in front of the house. When that comes up short, I walk over to the community center and cut to the basketball court behind the building, where, sure enough, a group of about a dozen boys are shouting, cheering, and bumping into one another. It looks like there are two different games going on both sides of the blacktop. Among the older players, I recognize Yasir and Mustafa, and Abdul and Shehzad—better known as Shezi—as boys I see around at the masjid. Kashif's with the younger boys, dribbling the ball with a determined look on his flushed face.

"Kashif!" I shout through the chain-link fence. When he doesn't hear me and continues playing, I yank the gate open and call out again with my hands cupping my mouth. "KASHIF! Amma says it's time to—!"

"Hey, heads up!"

I turn toward the voice, but all I catch sight of is the older boys' basketball slashing across the court like there's a bull's-eye on my face. I scream and am halfway to ducking, but someone charges in front of me and knocks the ball out of the air, sending it flying over my head to hit the fence with a metallic *thwump* instead.

Izyaan spins around to look at me, his bronze face and the front of his shirt drenched in sweat. "Ainy, are you okay? That was close!"

My hands are still covering my mouth in shock. Partly because I came *this* close to having my nose crushed, and partly because I wasn't expecting to run into Izyaan in my literal pajamas!

"You saved me," I say, low-key excitement humming in my stomach even though I almost conked out on the blacktop.

The other boys whoop and holler and clap. "Nice one, Izyaan!" one shouts. "You're her hero!" They fall all over themselves laughing and shoving one another.

My armpits are sweating and I think I need to take another shower.

"Ainy!" Finally, Kashif races up to me. "What are you doing here?"

"Looking for you," I say impatiently. "Time to go. Amma's waiting."

"Oh. Okay."

Izyaan catches my eye and smiles. I'm so glad I can blame the blush creeping up my neck on the blazing sun. I'm pretty sure my still-damp hair is hanging in loose, frizzy waves around my face. "See you around?" he asks.

"Yeah," I say. I wince inwardly and my stomach fills with butterflies as Izyaan fist-bumps Kashif and jogs back to his friends. *Way to make it awkward, Ainy.*

Kashif hollers to his buddies that he's leaving. I whirl to get a head start, but Yasir blocks my path to retrieve the ball sitting at the edge of the asphalt. He scoops up the ball, and as he passes me on the way back, his shoulder bumps mine, like he owns the court and shouldn't have to move aside for me.

"Nice shirt, Ainy," Yasir says, so close to my ear I can feel his hot breath on my cheek. "The unicorn's a *choice.*"

My throat closes up at the way Yasir stares pointedly at the prancing unicorn on my chest. I peek down at my white pajama shirt with the glittery pink-and-purple unicorn, wishing I could disappear. Now I *really* regret leaving the house in it.

I blink, but Yasir's already gone. He's never spoken two words to me, let alone looked at me, until today, and now he decides to talk to me twice in one day? I think back to how he asked me to sign his yearbook, which, now that I think about it, didn't have a ton of signatures when I flipped through it. If he was making people write next to their pictures, then I must've been one of the first ones . . . or one of the only ones. But why *me?*

Kashif tugs at my sleeve. "I like your shirt. Unicorns are cool!" he says, like Yasir had hurt my feelings. I can't tell if that's why I feel uneasy about the comment. Is it because he was calling me a baby for wearing something that looks like it belongs on a kid? It feels even weirder that he said that to me in front of my little brother.

I shake my head, vanquishing Yasir's molecules from my brain. I grab Kashif's hand and speed walk out of there. If these boys are planning on hanging around here all summer vacation, then I'm glad I have an excuse to be out of the house and away from them. I grin to myself.

Naseerah's Almari, here I come.

CHAPTER 4

Naseerah's Almari is located next to a sprawling parking garage in the growing town plaza fifteen minutes away. Amma's shop is on the ground floor of the building, which houses a massage therapist on the second floor and private offices on the third floor. Next door is a vintage shoe shop on one side and a bougie tea place on the other. The name *Naseerah's Almari*—Naseerah's Closet—fits because the front of the store is literally as big as a walk-in closet.

In other words, it's perfect.

"Ainy, you're gonna make yourself sick," Bajjo admonishes me.

I stop joy-spinning in the chair behind the counter, letting my stomach settle before flashing a huge grin. "Sorry. I'm just so happy! I can't believe I'm finally here."

Here, there's a dark blue counter that stretches from wall to wall with built-in swing doors on both sides. The thin carpet's a soft gray patterned with tiny gold stars. The front display window is decorated with current seasonal favorite pieces, which usually go fast, so Amma has to change it every few days. In the back is a storeroom that holds boxes, supplies in orderly bins and baskets, clothing racks, a sewing station, and an ironing and steaming stand. Unlike our house, the store is organized down to the last spool of thread.

It's my first day at work since school ended. Outside, the town center is busier than usual with kids and teenagers newly freed from the school year. After a long and boring semester, I need this. To be here, surrounded by clothes and a world of stylish possibilities.

Bajjo looks up from the computer at the other end of the counter. She's been typing away on it since we opened, looking cute in high-waisted pants and a pearly white silk hijab. I feel like a little kid trying to play dress-up next to her even though I tried extra hard to make a statement by copying one of my favorite content creator's Top 5 Modest Summer Looks. I'm in a summery yellow tulle romper, one of my favorite hand-me-downs from Bajjo because of how bright the color is. I paired it with black leggings sporting tiny rhinestones. The set of golden bangles glinting on my wrists are a gift Safiya brought back for me on her last trip to Pakistan.

"Come over here. I'm gonna teach you how to update the tracker," Bajjo says.

I push off the wall with my legs and wheel over to her. "What tracker?"

"It's a spreadsheet," says Bajjo. "It's got all our client names, contact info, pricing quotes, delivery timeline, et cetera. Super easy."

My jaw drops at the humongous list. Now I get why Amma hasn't taken a single break since we opened today. She's already turned in four pickups, answered the phone at least a half dozen times, did some cutting for a rush order, and now she's in the back taking a bride-to-be's measurements for her dress. Summer's all about weddings. That's why work has been picking up. I've just been watching and taking it all in, in a trance and trying not to get in the way, even though a hundred questions are crowding my brain.

"Where do you guys keep the fun stuff? In here?" I duck below the counter to scour through the shelves and cabinets underneath. They're filled with stacks of thick binders, sketchbooks, and Amma's slim tablet. Bingo.

"No touching!" Bajjo slaps my hand. I pull back with an offended look. "Training comes first. It's only your first day. You have to earn the right to do the fun stuff," Bajjo says in that I'm-older-so-listen-to-me voice. "You need to learn how to do all the basics so that we don't fall behind. I'm not going to be here to help all the time."

"Then why did you get another job at Aroma when there's already so much work to do here?" I ask, annoyed. Aroma is a trendy café that's a five-minute walk from here. The line there first thing in the morning is ridiculous.

Bajjo's eyes dart to the door leading to the back room and she lowers her voice. "Okay. Don't tell Amma I told you, but we need the extra money. For bills and stuff."

I blink at this. "What?"

"Yeah. We lost the insurance we had through Abu's company, and Amma's chipping in to help pay for Dadi's treatment. I'll be making a lot more at Aroma than I'm making here," Bajjo confesses. Her voice cracks a little. Bajjo's relationship with Dadi is different from mine. Dadi basically raised Bajjo from the time she was born in Pakistan until we moved to Virginia, and they actually stay in touch. I didn't stop to think how hard the cancer news must've been on my sister. "Don't worry. It's only for a little while. When Abu comes home, everything will go back to normal."

When's that? I want to ask but don't, because I don't want to sound like a whiny baby. My stomach drops and I try not to let my expression give me away. I signed up to learn how to design clothes, not sit around and do office work! But my grandmother has cancer and my mom and big sister are doing everything they can to help from all the way over here. Even Izyaan's parents are doing way more than I am, renting us their basement and looking after Kashif. The least I can do is not complain. If office work is what it's going to take to make my way up to the dream job, then I guess I don't have much of a choice. Especially if Amma's going to rely on me to keep things running smoothly when Bajjo's out.

"How hard can it be to work a computer?" I ask gleefully.

Turns out, it's not that easy. Bajjo walks me through the system: where important information is stored, what my spiel should be if I have to take a call while Amma's busy, pricing sheets ("NO haggling!"), inventory log and where we order supplies, where we keep receipts. By the end of her lecture, I'm cross-eyed.

"Don't worry. I wrote it all down for you." Bajjo proudly lifts up a binder that says AINY—TRAINING on it in looping purple Sharpie. "I know it sounds like a lot at first, but you'll get used to it. You might even get bored sometimes, so binge a show or read or something."

Oh, good. Hopefully that means my new full-time job won't get in the way of my and Safiya's summer plans. When I told Safiya I'm going to be working for Amma this summer, she said she was going to stop by on my first day to have lunch together. She already texted me five minutes ago to tell me she's on her way.

The back door opens and Amma emerges with her customers. Amma's measuring tape is dangling around her neck. She's always got it on her, the same way an artist might keep a pencil tucked behind their ear.

"Your groom will love it!" the older Arab woman gushes.

Amma looks directly at the younger woman, the bride. "But do *you* love it?" she asks.

The bride nods shyly, and I feel a surge of pride. My mom works super hard for this business. It's nice to know that people appreciate it. "If you have any questions, please let me know."

Safiya waltzes in with an exaggerated flourish as the two women leave the store.

"That one is *so* cute," she says, pointing at the intricate pink-and-orange gharara displayed in the window.

"Salaam, Safiya. I knew you'd like that one," Amma says, neatly winding her measuring tape around her finger. "Very much your style."

"Look at you!" Safiya gushes, holding up her fingers like she's taking a snapshot of me. "Ainy Zain. Future fashion designer. The reason why I will never have to worry about what to wear ever again." I laugh. "Are you ready?" Safiya continues. "I'm starving."

"Go ahead," Bajjo says. She doesn't look up from her phone as she scrolls endlessly. "We'll cover more after lunch."

"More what?" Safiya asks as I grab my purse and walk out of the store with her. Safiya's arm presses into mine as she leans into me. "Top secret design lessons? Spill!"

I sigh. "No. I wish." At Safiya's raised eyebrow I add, "I'm not allowed to help with the actual designing work yet. I have to learn the front desk first."

"Huh? Why?"

I shrug as we make our way down the shop-lined street. "Bajjo got a new job because it's more money. That's why Amma hired me. Because she needs me to take over Bajjo's old responsibilities, not because she thinks I'm good enough to help her with designing clothes." Saying it out loud makes me wilt.

"That's so not true!" Safiya exclaims, startling a man and the baby strapped to his chest who are walking past us. "You're an amazing designer. Remember the outfit I ordered online last year for my mom's cousin's wedding?"

I shudder. "That dress was so ugly."

"Yeah! And I cried so much because I didn't have time to buy a new one. Then you saved the day with, like, pins and scissors and border trim and turned it into one of my favorite fits! I still have it. So, don't you dare doubt yourself, Ainy Zain. I forbid it."

I smile weakly. Safiya's right. I do have what it takes to be an awesome designer. I'm just disappointed because I was hoping to finally learn more about design from Amma, but maybe if I learn quickly and become an expert assistant like Bajjo, I'll eventually have enough free time to spend with Amma so that she can mentor me. I already got the job. Now I just need to be patient.

"Thanks, Safi," I say.

"No problem. And when you do start making beautiful dresses, I want you to design something specially for me."

"Deal!" The smell of food hits me as we enter our favorite halal burger joint and my mouth waters. The place is so packed, the room sounds like it's buzzing with a swarm of bees. "I hope we can find a table," I say as we wend through the crowd, careful not to trip on people's bags.

"We can always try to find room in the plaza. Oh, found one!" Safiya spots two empty seats at the end of a full table near the other entrance. Except . . .

I stop in my tracks. "What are *they* doing here?"

Yasir and his friends from the basketball court are at the table eating and horsing around.

Safiya grabs my arms and whispers gleefully, "Ainy, look! There's *Izyaan*. Let's go say hi!"

Before I can open my mouth to protest, she's pushing me in their direction, announcing, "What up, everyone?" and there's nothing I can do once the boys see us approaching.

Izyaan throws one arm on the back of his chair and waves at me and Safiya with the other. "Hey! Fancy seeing you guys here."

Safiya sways closer to me. "Ainy here is working at her mom's store this summer. Naseerah's Almari. You know the one?" Safiya winks at me. She mouths, *I got you!*

I freeze up. My heart is speeding and not in a good way. Why did she have to tell them that? Now they all know where I'm going to be. The others exchange knowing glances around the table. My whole body's acting funny, like it wants me to flee. But that's ridiculous. You run from danger, not stupid boys your own age.

Izyaan brightens. "I already knew that, but that's cool! Wanna sit? We ordered a lot of food."

I might like Izyaan a lot, but that doesn't mean I should be hanging out with him and his friends for no reason. I know what my boundaries are with boys, and this one's—

"Don't mind if we do!" Safiya flops into the chair across from Izyaan and helps herself to some curly fries, taking them out from right under Mustafa's nose. That leaves me with the seat next to Izyaan. Stuck, I realize I'm still standing and quickly sit down but scooch a little so our elbows don't touch. Izyaan passes me an unwrapped slider.

"So, what's new with you?" I ask him to make up for our intrusion. "Got any special summer plans?"

"Hi," Shezi grunts. "We're sitting here, too."

Safiya slides him a disgusted glare. "She wasn't talking to you."

Yasir, Mustafa, and Abdul snicker. I swear, Kashif's more mature than this.

"Anyways," I say, my cheeks growing hot again when I see Mustafa catch Yasir's eye and snicker. "Your plans?"

Izyaan smiles. "Right. Mostly classes and competitions." He means competitive fencing classes. Izyaan's been playing the sport since he was seven, and he's really good. "What about you? Sounds like Kashif's going to be spending a lot of time at my place."

"You should come play basketball with us," Yasir interrupts. He sits up straighter and puffs out his chest. "I can teach you. That way you don't get creamed next time Shezi completely misses his shot."

Safiya scrunches up her face. Her eyes bore into mine like, *You didn't tell me about that.*

"No, thanks," I say flatly. I'd rather eat worms. Yasir's smile disappears and the others pretend like they had the wind knocked out of them.

"Sorry, Yasir." Abdul chuckles. "Looks like Ainy would rather hang out with Izyaan. His face is nicer than yours anyway. Can't blame her!"

I want to hide behind the soda fountain machine.

"Knock it off," Izyaan growls like he's genuinely annoyed. My ribs pinch. Did he say that because he wants his friends to stop teasing me or *him*? Does he know I like him like that? Is he embarrassed?

"Oh, would you look at the time!" Safiya stands abruptly. "Break's over. C'mon, Ainy. We don't want your mom to fire you on your first day. Thanks for the food, guys! This was great. We should do it again sometime." Safiya comes around and flips me out of my chair. I catch myself before I land in Izyaan's lap. "Bye!" she calls out to them. Then she steers me out of the diner like I'm a remote-controlled car. When we're out of earshot she mutters, "Psych. I hope they choke on their fries. Bunch of morons."

"You went up to them first!"

"Only because I want you and Prince Izyaan to live happily ever after!"

I turn beet red. "Subtle is not your thing, you know that?"

"What was up with Yasir?" Safiya gives me a questioning look like I know something she doesn't. "He was acting so weird."

"How should I know?" I ask.

Safiya leans into my ear and whispers, "You don't think it's possible that Yasir likes you—AHHH!" She jerks away when I snatch at her and busts out laughing.

"Take that back!" I screech.

"I'm kidding, I'm kidding!" Safiya squeals, and takes off running through the town square as I give chase, waving my fist in the air, shouting, "You better be!"

CHAPTER 5

Bajjo opens and closes the drawer behind the counter so aggressively that it rattles above my head. I hoist myself up from the floor, where I've been organizing magazines and catalogs all afternoon, to see Bajjo drop her phone and wallet into her purse.

"Amma!" she calls out. "I'm taking twenty. Ainy's in charge of the front desk."

My mouth opens in protest. "Who, me?"

"It's good practice," Bajjo says in a businesslike voice. "For when I'm not here all day and you have to step up. Besides, wasn't working here your idea?"

"And you're supposed to be teaching me how, not making me sit here recycling old magazines!" I bite back.

"I've been training you all day, and I can't show you

how to deal with customers when there are no customers," Bajjo retorts. The store's been dead ever since Safiya left after lunch. Amma hasn't moved from her place in the back, and Bajjo has been answering emails or checking her phone while I was bored out of my mind cleaning out the shelves.

I press my hands over my eyes to calm down. Bajjo's been in a weird mood ever since I got back. She didn't even thank me when I brought her her favorite milkshake as a treat, even though I think putting Almond Joy in anything is a crime! It's an offense to candy everywhere. I don't know what's up with her. Ever since she started high school, there's always some drama going on in Bajjo's life. Maybe she got into a fight with Amarah?

Bajjo looks at her phone again. A storm brews behind her eyes. "Be back soon," she clips out before turning to leave.

Alone, I blow a raspberry and sink into the computer chair. Definitely some kind of friend drama going on. Maybe if Bajjo cools down by the time we get home, she'll tell me about it. She always does. If anything is preparing me for the horrors of becoming a teenager, it's Bajjo's stories.

I spend the next five minutes cleaning up the mess I made. Once the recycling bin is full and the shelf is stocked with only the most up-to-date magazine issues for research purposes, I inspect the checklist Bajjo keeps on the computer's Notes app. My eyes skip over all the managerial work, my brain begging for a drop of creativity, when I see it. Near the bottom of the list is an unfinished task that reads ZIA ENGAGEMENT DRESS DESIGN.

I pull up the tracker to investigate and my eyes widen. It's due in five days! Has Amma even started working on it yet? Too curious for my own good now, I make sure Amma's tied up in the back before sneakily opening the cabinet to take out her tablet. Just a tiny peek, I promise myself. I deserve it after the best day of my life went downhill faster than a broken bicycle. Using the stylus, I swipe through the alphabetized folders by client name, searching for *Zia*. Amma brainstorms all her initial ideas in here, so if she *has* already started designing—

Aha! I tap on the folder labeled *Zia* and a curvy, faceless figure fills the screen. Amma uses software with this cool feature where she can input all the customer's measurements and the figure—the croquis—will automatically adjust its size. She can even move the limbs around into different poses like a digital doll. So far, the model has basic strokes outlining an A-line dress with scattered marks noting where certain embellishments are going to go. And . . . that's all. It's nowhere near complete.

I scratch the back of my head with the stylus, contemplating. *Well, I'm supposed to make sure Amma doesn't fall behind. This counts as making sure she stays on track.* My hand comes alive on its own and sets the very tip of the pen on top of the screen, right in the center of the skirt. I can't explain why, but this one's got to have an asymmetric hemline. No, wait. High-low! And the shalwar needs embroidered ruffles to give it that almost-a-bride-but-not-quite look. I grin, imagining Amma's face when she realizes that I was the one who came up with the idea all by myself. She'll be blown away, and she'll be so grateful for my help that she won't be able to resist making me her official design assistant. Then everything will take a turn for the better again.

"Cute dress," says a low voice.

I gasp, my hand skidding across the screen. A thick black brushstroke blots out Amma's illustration like spilled ink.

No, no, no! Heart racing, I frantically hit the undo button—thank *God* I didn't save over it—and snap the case closed. My gaze jumps up to meet Yasir standing on the other side of the counter, his nose hovering inches above the tablet. Inches from where *my* face was a second ago. Mustafa, Abdul, and Shezi are fanned out in a line behind him. They wave at me smugly. It's just the four of them.

Where did Izyaan go?

Yasir leans one arm on the counter, nodding toward the tablet. "Was that for you? Beats the unicorn pajamas."

The other boys chuckle. Suddenly, the temperature inside the store skyrockets to a hundred degrees. I feel woozy.

"Don't look so weirded out, Ainy. It was a compliment." Yasir cocks his head at me, like he's trying to tell me two things at the same time.

"What he's trying to say is that you're pretty," Abdul clarifies, looking smug. Yasir flicks his friend's ear but doesn't look embarrassed about being exposed.

Wait, he thinks I'm pretty?

You don't think it's possible that Yasir likes you? Safiya's voice echoes inside my head. No. No way. Safiya had been joking! I mean, who *acts* like this in front of their crush?

This can't be happening. Maybe if I close my eyes I can pretend none of this is real. Magically teleport myself to a Yasir-free zone.

"U-um, thanks," I stutter, because what else am I supposed to respond? Mustafa, Abdul, and Shezi leave Yasir at the counter to wander around the store, but they obviously don't get too far. Even though none of them are looking in my direction, I sense all their attention on me anyway. Me and Yasir. It feels like being trapped in a cage with hungry tigers.

"You're really going to be stuck here all summer?" Mustafa asks, wrinkling his nose as he roams around the small store. "Did you get in trouble?"

"No." My cheeks warm indignantly. "I offered to help. I want to be a designer like my mom. Hey, don't touch that!" I scold Shezi when I see him rubbing our window mannequin's kurta between his fingers. I'm ninety-five percent sure that boy doesn't wash his hands.

Shezi shrugs but drops his hand. "Just looking."

"We're going to watch a movie at the Alamo. You should come, too," says Yasir, and my eyes jut out of their sockets. He can't be serious. Yasir's parents are two of the most influential people in our community. His dad is a big-shot Realtor. And his mom? Two words: gossipy auntie. The only reason they're on the masjid board, the one Abu was on, too, before he had to leave, is because so much of our masjid's state-of-the-art facility comes from their family's donations. People are always tripping over their own feet to please them like they're royalty. Keeping up a good image is everything to Yasir's parents. He wouldn't be caught dead talking to a girl in front of them, let alone asking her out. What if somebody saw us together? Not that I would *ever* agree to watch a movie with Yasir and his cronies. I'd rather poke myself with a needle a dozen times.

Yasir raps his knuckles on the counter while I'm spaced out. "Yoo-hoo. Ainy. You still in there?"

"I'm good, thanks. I mean, you guys go ahead. I have to work," I say, hating how weak I sound.

"But you're not doing anything right now," Yasir points out.

I gesture awkwardly at the computer monitor. "I have to finish up this order thing," I splutter. As if to emphasize my point, I snatch the wireless mouse and start clicking on random tabs to look busy, staring hard at the screen. If I keep ignoring him, he's sure to take the hint that I'm not interested and leave.

"Boring. Okay, fine. What about tomorrow?"

The hair on the back of my neck stands up. *Tomorrow? He's planning on coming back?*

"She would've said yes if Izyaan was still here," Abdul

says. Yasir shoots him a dark look, but Abdul smirks at me. "You like Izzy, don't you, Ainy? We *told* Yasir he didn't stand a chance—OW!" Abdul rubs the shoulder Yasir punched to shut him up and scowls.

I stop breathing for a split second before Bajjo's training finally kicks in and tackles my nerves to the ground. "Do you need me to get my mom? She's the clothes expert. Not me."

"Your mom's here?" Yasir straightens and the others not-so-subtly back up.

"Yeah," I say more boldly. I hook a thumb over my shoulder. "She's in there."

Yasir starts walking away from the counter, the other three a few steps ahead of him. "All right, we won't bother you anymore. Catch you later, Ainy! Let me know if you change your mind!" He titters before spinning in a circle and joining his friends. Their annoying laughter reaches my ears until they're out of sight through the window.

You wish, I think, breathing a huge sigh of relief as the back room door clicks open and Amma peeks out. She blinks like she's seeing the sun for the first time in days. "Who were you talking to, Ainy?" she asks. "Was that a customer?"

"No one," I say quickly, trying to cover up my flustered appearance. "Just watching a video Safiya sent me."

But I'm on edge for the rest of the day, and I can't help but stress out about whether Yasir might show up again. Like he could still be around, biding his time. Waiting to corner me.

CHAPTER 6

I bite off the last length of thread from the seams of an old shirt and shake it off over the side of my bed to inspect my handiwork. *Not bad, Zain.* The front reads OH, YOU LIKE MY OUTFIT? THANKS, IT'S DESIGNER. Abu got it for me a long time ago. I forgot all about it until I found it at the bottom of my drawer when I'd run out of clean clothes. It was too tight across my chest when I tried it on. Since there was enough room—gunjaish, as Amma would say in Urdu—to loosen it up, I grabbed my sewing kit and went for it. I like doing easy alterations every now and then so my skills don't turn rusty.

Besides, I needed the distraction after today.

I'm going to have to go shopping soon, though. I'm not super tall or anything, but I hit a growth spurt this year. Amma and Bajjo took me to get my first training bra when the doctor announced I'd started "developing" (it was as mortifying as it sounds). And now that I've hit puberty, I'm required to cover my awrah in public. Amma suggested I should really look at my wardrobe and start thinking about what makes me comfortable. The way she said it sounded like a riddle, which means it's code for modest. Obviously, she wants me to dress modestly because that's what Islam encourages. Kashif doesn't even wear shorts because boys have to cover past their knees.

But I'm one step ahead. I reach down and use my foot to slowly open my creaky nightstand. Sitting perfectly folded right at the top of all my junk is my little secret. The scarf is teal green—my favorite color—and slightly crinkled, with a hint of shimmer. My first-day hijab. I made it myself. I found the leftover fabric in Amma's stuff and fell in love with the material. I couldn't let it go to waste. The scarf has been sitting here for a few months, waiting for me to finally put it to good use. And I will. Soon . . .

A slight hiccuping noise draws my attention across the room, to where Bajjo is making dua after reading salat. I called dibs earlier and went first. That corner is the only space in our bedroom where we can pray without hitting our heads or our butts on a piece of furniture.

"Look at this!" I say, holding up the T-shirt proudly to Bajjo once she spreads her hands down her face. She slowly looks over her right shoulder at me and I balk at her watery eyes. Is she *crying*?

"Bajjo, are you—?" I start anxiously.

"Wow, that old thing?" Bajjo interrupts me. She uses her sleeve to wipe her nose and drops her headscarf onto the prayer rug, revealing her long, dark brown hair. "I can't believe you still have it."

"Yeah," I say, eyeing her carefully. Bajjo smiles, but her face kind of looks like what it might if a dog pooped on her shoes. My sister never cries. Not even when she loses a debate, and Bajjo *hates* losing. I'm worried something really bad happened. Immediately, I think of Dadi and dread sets my nerves on fire.

Before I can open my mouth to try asking her again, Kashif yells frustratingly from the kitchen. "Ainy! What's wrong with this thing?"

Sighing, I close my drawer, toss the shirt aside, and jump off my bed to go see what all the commotion is. In the galley kitchen, Kashif's glaring at the stove with his hands on his hips. "I can hear it lighting, but it won't turn on!" he whines.

"The plate's probably blocking the flames. Here." I adjust the burner plate, and next time, it blazes to life.

Kashif, the human equivalent of a floppy-eared bunny, hops up and down ecstatically. "Finally!"

I eye the ingredients next to the stove. "What are you making? We already ate dinner."

"I'm still hungry. Amma said I could make a sandwich."

"Do you need a hand?" Bajjo asks, coming up behind me. "I can—"

"No!" Kashif and I exclaim in unison. Everything Bajjo touches in the kitchen dies or catches fire. It's safer for everyone if she doesn't get involved. We trust Kashif more and he's only nine.

"Wow, guys. *Fine,*" Bajjo huffs. She turns her nose up and stomps out to where Amma is sitting in the living room. I hope Aroma doesn't fire Bajjo after one day.

"Want one?" Kashif offers me, using the spatula to put two slices of bread on the pan. "It's a cheesy melt."

"Isn't that just grilled cheese?"

"No," he snaps like I'm being offensive. "This has tomatoes."

"Same thing." I cross my ankles and watch him make

grilled cheese. "So, what did you do upstairs all day?" I ask stealthily. "You must've been pretty bored."

Kashif shrugs. "Not really. Izyaan bhai went out and he let me play games. Sister Ambreen made a lot of snacks. Mostly, I hung out with Cocoa." Cocoa is the Khalids' gray-and-white Ragdoll. Kashif treats that cat like a baby. "Oh, and I played basketball."

"With who?" I drill him.

"Dante and Ajay. I always play with them."

"Good." Izyaan by himself is fine—Kashif adores Izyaan—but the thought of my little brother hanging out with the other boys makes my stomach churn unpleasantly. "Stick to your own friends. You don't have to hang around the older boys."

"You're not the boss of me," says Kashif, tearing the plastic off a slice of cheese and flipping it onto one of the toasting bread pieces.

I want to say *I'm older so actually yeah I am* but I know that won't go over so well. I don't want to sound like I'm getting on his case, but I can't ignore the disturbing feeling in the pit of my stomach. Yasir and his goons are not allowed to rub off on my little brother. I'd rather Kashif spend all his time snuggling Cocoa.

"Whatever. Don't forget to turn off the stove," I

instruct, strolling out of the kitchen to see what Amma and Bajjo are up to. I skid to a halt in the living room when I see them talking to Sister Ambreen and Amarah. I didn't hear them come downstairs. They're both hijab-less because Kashif hasn't hit puberty yet, so it's okay if he sees them with their hair down. Bajjo snatches Amarah's wrist and tugs her into our bedroom like the rest of us don't exist.

"Salaam, Ainy," Sister Ambreen greets me with a warm smile. Normally, I would call Izyaan and Amarah's mom Ambreen Auntie, but she's been teaching at our Sunday school for so long that "Sister Ambreen" stuck.

"I came down to get your laundry," says Sister Ambreen. Right. I forgot. We don't have a unit in the basement, so Sister Ambreen, Amarah, or Izyaan will come downstairs to get our loads once a week. I used to purposely leave my butterfly-patterned underwear out of the pile if Izyaan was the one to come pick it up. Learned my lesson when I ran out of clean underwear one time. Having your crush live upstairs is not the dream scenario it sounds like.

"I'll get it," I offer, and mosey over to the bathroom to grab the basket of dirty clothes by the shower tub. I remember the smelly pair of socks at the foot of my bed, too, and go back to my room for them. Bajjo and Amarah are in there, sitting on Bajjo's bed and talking in low voices. I overhear Bajjo muttering things like "it's not fair" and "can't catch a break" under her breath. Amarah's mouth is twisted to one side as if she's trying to work something out. They're in a sour mood, and both fall silent when they notice me.

I stand there for a few seconds, thinking Bajjo will loop me in, but she looks like she's waiting for me to leave instead. My face starts to heat up the longer they pretend like I didn't walk in on what was obviously a private conversation.

"Need something?" Bajjo finally asks.

"It's my room, too," I stammer out instead of *what were you whispering about?* Irritation pricks at me like needles. Since when did I become the annoying little sister? I get that Amarah is Bajjo's best friend, but I'm not the one who should feel embarrassed or left out. But lately, it's like Bajjo would rather hang out with Amarah than with me. Even now, Bajjo clearly doesn't want to clue me in. I pluck my socks off the floor and turn out of there, trying not to stomp my feet like a baby.

"Jazakallah, Ainy," Sister Ambreen says when I bring her the laundry basket.

"I wish you would let me take it to a laundromat instead of having you do an extra chore," Amma says softly. "You're already doing so much for us, and now you're babysitting Kashif, too." She's sitting cross-legged against the sofa with her sewing machine and a green embroidered kameez draped across her lap. Pieces of frayed cloth and tangled thread litter the space around her, and her hair is falling out of its braid.

"Naseerah, I've told you it's no trouble," Sister Ambreen says modestly. "Besides, the machine does all the work. I can hardly take credit. And you know how much I adore Kashif."

I smile appreciatively at Sister Ambreen. If it weren't for the Khalids letting us live with them so that Abu could go to Pakistan, we'd be out on the streets. Our own family in Texas doesn't know about our situation. Even if they did, I'm one hundred percent sure they wouldn't care. They already think they did us a huge favor by bringing us to America. But the Khalids didn't look the other way. Sister Ambreen's been more caring and helpful than Amma's own sister. This is her house, but she lets us have our privacy in the basement as if it's our own.

"How's your new job?" Sister Ambreen asks me.

"Great!" I say, making my best fake happy face and quickly steering the conversation away from me working at the store. "Are you excited about teaching that class this summer? The Women in Islam one?"

"Oh yes. It finally got approved this year, alhamdulillah. Spread the word for me. It's open to everyone, not just girls. I'm encouraging boys to sign up, too. Though rumor has it not everyone is pleased with that idea."

"Who is giving you a hard time?" asks Amma.

"Who do you think?" Sister Ambreen rolls her eyes. "God forbid we teach our boys to learn and respect female contributions to society."

Amma and Sister Ambreen don't say another word because they don't like to gossip behind people's backs, but I know exactly who they're talking about. Gabina Auntie. Yasir's mom. She's a cultural nutjob, as Bajjo likes to put it.

"She pretends like she's so religious when she's really just backward," Bajjo said to me one time. "It's embarrassing how much people kiss that family's feet for money." Sometimes I can't believe Sister Ambreen, Amarah, and Izyaan are related to them. Sister Ambreen and her husband are the exact opposite of her brother and his wife. Everyone knows who really has the community's best interests at heart, but no one has the guts to call Gabina Auntie out. I'm actually scared of her.

"Well, I'll be on my way with these. Amarah! Let's go!" says Sister Ambreen. "Call me if you need anything, Naseerah," she adds when Amarah comes bounding out with a grim-looking Bajjo trailing behind her. Amarah pats Bajjo's shoulders and wraps her in a quick hug—it shouldn't annoy me, but it does—before following her mom upstairs.

"Amma, give it a rest," Bajjo chides her when it's just us again. "You've been at it all day."

Amma sighs and rubs her eyes tiredly. "There aren't enough hours in the day," she says, sounding wiped out. "I'm so grateful I have you two to help."

"Don't worry. Ainy'll catch up in no time and everything will get easier, in shaa Allah." Bajjo throws one arm around my shoulder cheerily. I side-eye her at the sudden mood switch from a moment ago. "You can count on us, Amma."

"Yeah," I murmur. It's hitting me now just how much Amma is counting on me. Then my mind wanders to a certain boy with greasy brown eyes who's used to getting what he wants. This time's different, though. I'm not going to let Yasir intimidate me out of working at

Naseerah's Almari when my family needs me. Never in a million years.

All I have to do is ignore him. At some point, he's going to have to accept that I'm never going to like him the same way and back off. I just have to be patient.

CHAPTER 7

As slow as the store was yesterday, it was nonstop *go go go* today. Deliveries, taking new orders, fittings, answering phone calls, correcting mishaps. Amma did a design consultation that Bajjo let me sit in on to watch, and the whole time I had to keep my mouth pinched between my fingers so I wouldn't butt in with suggestions.

By the end of the day, my bones felt like they were made of jelly. But now it's the middle of the night and I can't sleep. Tomorrow is Bajjo's first day at her new job and I'm going to be managing the front desk by myself until after lunch. I keep imagining everything that can go wrong without Bajjo and it turns me into bundle of nerves.

The room feels empty tonight even though Bajjo is

ten feet away, sound asleep in her own bed. It's like all the warmth has been sucked dry from the air, leaving me shivering underneath my blanket. We worked together all day but that's all that we talked about. Work.

Suddenly, I miss Abu so much it twists my gut. I slide my phone out from under my pillow and check the time. It's past midnight here, so the day's just getting started in Karachi. Quietly, I wiggle out of bed so I don't disturb Bajjo but end up landing on the floor with an *oomph!* all tangled up in my blanket. I fumble through the dark, crawling out of our bedroom and through the kitchen into the weak night-light of the living room. Kashif's tucked in on the pull-out sofa. He sleeps like the dead, so I don't have to worry about him waking up.

I sit as close to the little bit of light as possible at the dining table before tapping on my phone to video call Abu. I don't think he's going to pick up, but when it actually connects and Abu's gentle face and thick beard fill my phone screen, my eyes start to burn with tears.

"Asalamualaikum. Arey Quratulain beta, isn't it late? What are you doing still awake?" Abu's sitting in front of the iron-grated window in my dadi's bedroom, the bright sun at the back of his head. It's been two months since Abu left to go to Pakistan—only a month after Naseerah's

Almari's grand opening—but sometimes it feels like he's been gone for years. Abu's the most reserved out of all of us, but he's always been our safety net. Like no matter what happened, everything would be all right as long as he was there.

"Walaikumusalam, Abu," I say. "Couldn't sleep. What are you doing? How's Dadi?"

"I'm reading Qur'an. Your dadi is sleeping right here. I have to make sure she takes her medicine on time."

"Oh." I fall silent, noticing that he sort of ignored my question.

"Tell me about the business. Your amma's been going on to me about how fast you're learning the ropes. I'm so proud of you!"

I snort and sink lower in my chair. Amma is exaggerating. We all know I'm a slow learner. Bajjo yelled at me at least three times for getting things wrong today. It was a stressful shift overall.

Abu reads the look on my face with concern. "What's going on, Ainy? You look troubled."

"When are you coming home?"

Abu's gaze softens at the catch in my voice. "I don't know yet, beta. Your dadi needs me here. It could be a while."

But we need you, too. I wipe at the stupid tears building in my eyes with the sleeve of my shirt. I ask the question that's been sitting in the pit of my stomach for weeks. "Abu, how bad is it? Is Dadi going to be okay? Be honest."

Abu's expression droops at my question, making him appear almost ten years older. I hold my breath, bracing for bad news.

"The doctors fear that the cancer might have spread," he finally admits. My whole body goes rigid. "They're going to run more tests to find out where and how much."

"Does Amma know? Can they treat it if it has spread?" There's an almost desperate ring to my words now.

"Yes, I already told your mother. We will know more in the next few days, in shaa Allah," Abu says. He sighs deeply like he's crumbling inside. "Please make lots of dua for your dadi's health. Give sadaqah in her name."

That explains why the circles underneath Amma's eyes have looked darker recently. I thought it was just because she was working around the clock.

I grip the edge of the table with one hand. "I wish there was something I could do."

"You are helping, beta. By helping your amma and Bajjo with the business, you're doing more than you realize. Take care of them. I know your mom and sister.

They will both work themselves into the ground if there's nobody there to keep them up."

Guilt gnaws at my stomach. I *didn't* join the store to help my family. I did it because I wanted to learn how to be a better designer. I didn't ask to be the glue holding my family together.

"You should go to sleep now," Abu says. "You don't want to be tired for work tomorrow."

"Yeah. Okay," I say glumly. I've never felt so useless. "Talk to you later."

"In shaa Allah. Allah hafiz, beta."

Abu ends the call and I drop my phone on the table, tugging at my hair with trepidatious fingers. This was going to be the best summer vacation ever, but nothing's going the way it was supposed to. At least Safiya's parents agreed to drop Safiya off at the store whenever she wants, so that we can spend more time together. They did today while they took Noor to the park. Safiya seemed kind of disgruntled by my lack of attention toward her. It was one busy shift, though. Our summer plans haven't changed. There's still plenty of time for all that.

My phone screen suddenly lights up on the table. I stare at it for half a second before picking it up and swiping down to check my notifications. My tongue turns to rubber when I read the name.

Yasir. How did he get my number?!

I open the message and my chest relaxes when I see that it's through Scope—our countywide school social media app. It's the only platform Amma will let me have an account on since posts are monitored and only students are on it. There are also a bunch of different groups, committees, and forums you can join if you're in the same class, club, or sport as your fellow peers. I didn't think Yasir and I were in any of the same groups, but looking now, I see that there's one we do have in common—*Rising Seventh Graders.* Safiya and Izyaan are in it, too. Guess that should be a no-brainer. I bet everyone in my grade joined this group. Some people are already talking about what teachers they want next year, while others are posting vacation pictures like school's the last thing they want to think about. I'm squarely on Team Done with School.

I wait like Yasir's message will magically disappear on its own if I don't open it. I *could* delete it and pretend like I never received it. But I'm almost positive Yasir will bug me until I do respond, and I don't want him to have a reason to talk to me in person. I was on edge the whole day at work, thinking Yasir would stay true to his word about coming by again, but luckily, he didn't show. That doesn't mean he's going to stay away forever, though. Somehow, I just know I haven't seen the last of him.

Steeling myself upright, I open the message.

> Hey, Ainy, sorry I missed ya today. The store looked really busy anyway. I tried waving at you through the window but you didn't see me.

I read the message again, my heart pounding. So, it wasn't in my head after all. Yasir *had* been there. Watching me like a total creep. And now he has the guts to message me like we're pals? Doesn't he have any idea how wrong that is? Sweat slicks my fingertips as I consider what to do. I know I shouldn't respond. Just ignore him and then he'll leave me alone, right?

I look down at Yasir's message again and can't help myself. He's not getting off that easy.

Before I know it, I'm typing a reply.

> **Me:** I never told you to come.
> **Yasir:** Whoa, chill out. So I'm not even allowed to say hi to you?

Me: What for? We're not friends.

Yasir: Not yet :)

I gag. Wow. Talk about a big head.

Me: Not ever. Besides, we're not allowed to be friends.

Yasir: Says who? Because I'm a boy? I know you don't actually follow that dumb religious rule. You're friends with Izyaan.

My nostrils flare. I almost argue that that's not true, but I can also see why he might think that.

Me: No, our families are.

Yasir: I know. That's why you're living in his basement.

I stiffen, an uncomfortable feeling sinking in my stomach. It's not like it's a secret that my family moved in here, but I don't like Yasir knowing my family's private matters. Of course he's going to know, whether I like it or not, because of Gabina Auntie. Sister Ambreen wouldn't keep our living arrangements a secret from her own sister-in-law. The thought of Yasir visiting the Khalids and literally standing right above my head sends a spidery feeling crawling up my arms.

You still there? Yasir adds when I don't answer right away.

I gotta go. Bye, I say, too exhausted to keep having this conversation. I power my phone's screen off.

I carefully feel my way back to my room in the dark and lie down, staring across the space at Bajjo's sleeping form. I've never been liked by a boy before, and I never imagined it would be like this. Or that it would be Yasir of all people. Bajjo might be acting funky, but she's still the one person whose opinion I trust the most. Tomorrow when she comes in for work at the store after her other job, I'll ask for her advice on what I should do about Yasir. How I can get him off my back.

Bajjo'll have the answer. She always does.

CHAPTER 8

—

Safiya's eyes are wide, her mouth hanging open in a silent gasp. "Tell your mom sorry, but I'm stealing all of these. Oh, and I work here now."

She hip bumps me out of the way to dig through the boxes the delivery guy just dropped off at the shop. Vendors send Amma samples of new products to test out all the time. They contain everything from the latest prints and fabrics to seasonal must-haves and sewing supplies. Lucky for us, business has been a slow trickle today, so Safiya and I pounced on all the goods the minute they arrived.

"Mine!" Safiya cackles, snatching the first packet out of my hands. It's the monthly feature fabric. The material wrapped inside the plastic is a gorgeous jewel pink.

"Hey, no fair! I saw it first!" I laugh, reaching for it with grabby hands.

"Too slow." Safiya carefully peels the plastic open and unfolds the cloth on the counter. It has a netted quality to it, but it's thicker than tulle. The fabric stretches about a yard long and feels buttery smooth between my fingers. Bonus: It's not even a tiny bit scratchy.

"Yes," Safiya says dreamily, drawing out the word as she caresses the cloth to her cheek. "So soft."

I let Safiya have her moment, happy that she's cheerier today than yesterday. I shift my attention to the rest of the contents. There's a travel-size pouch, a few different-colored fabric markers, satin ribbons, a magnetic wrist pincushion, a packet of cute buttons, a catalog, and a sheet of stickers just for kicks. Looking through all the free-bies makes me feel charged after the crappy night I had. I barely slept, my mind turning over Bajjo's strangeness and what Abu told me and Yasir's messages. Bajjo left for Aroma before us, so I didn't get to see her this morning. My attention keeps drawing to the time, waiting for her shift to be up so I can talk to her about Yasir. Until I get it off my chest, the antsiness underneath my skin won't leave me alone.

Safiya and I haul the boxes to the back room. For

once, Amma isn't cutting or sewing or measuring anything. Instead, she's at her cramped desk flipping through a magazine, her niqab flipped out of her face. Her tablet is balanced on her knees. She looks relaxed for the first time in ages.

"Naseerah Auntie, check this out." Safiya wraps the pink cloth around her shoulders like a short cape and twirls on one foot.

"Oh, this will drape like a dream," Amma says, reaching out to touch it.

"I have a scarf that would look amazing with this color," Safiya crows. She knows how to style her hijab just right with every outfit. It's as easy as pie for her. She's always been comfortable in hijab since the first day she showed up with it on in public. I haven't really shared with her that I want to be a hijabi, too. It just feels like something I should keep to myself until it actually happens. I don't want to make promises, then get cold feet and look like a quitter.

I crane my neck to take a peek at what Amma's working on. "Who's that for?"

"For Noor, actually," says Amma. "Safiya's mom asked me for an aqeeqah outfit. I work on it between projects to unwind a bit since there's no rush."

Safiya wrinkles her nose like Amma said something offensive. The aqeeqah is a ceremony that takes place after a baby is born. Meat from an animal is sacrificed and shared with family and friends, usually within the first week. A lot of people have a party to welcome the baby, too, but sometimes it gets pushed to later. Noor's aqeeqah is going to be in August so that friends and family from out of town can make it.

"I can't believe my parents still want to do that," Safiya fusses. "She'll be seven months old by then! Who's going to care at that point?" Safiya doesn't even call her sister Noor. It's always "the baby" or "that smelly, drooling critter." I think Noor's cute, but I try not to dote on her too much in front of Safiya because I know how Safiya gets.

To my utter delight, Amma flips her tablet around to show me her sketches. "I'm leaning toward an anarkali cut. It'll look so precious." I'm already changing it up in my head before Amma's done talking. I know what she's getting at, but it still needs a little pizzazz. That's my problem. For me, every single design *has* to look like it's going to win the award for Best Dress.

"What about a waistcoat?" I suggest. "Safiya, what do you think—?" But when I turn around, there's only air. Somewhere in the middle of my and Amma's conversation about Noor's dress, Safiya left to go back to the front of the store. I duck my head through the door and spot her sitting idly behind the counter.

As much as I want to stick around and talk design with Amma a little longer, I don't want to abandon my best friend when she's upset.

"Hey, what's wrong?" I ask, sidling up to her.

"Noor," Safiya says through her teeth. "I can't escape her even when I'm with you."

"But she's not here—"

"Yes, she is!" Safiya exclaims. "She's everywhere. Everything is Noor this, Noor that. Sometimes it feels like I don't even exist. Even my grandparents and aunts and uncles don't pay as much attention to me anymore, and if they do it's *always* to ask me how I'm liking being a big sister." Safiya snorts. "She won't last five minutes in that dress before pooping all over it. Mark my words."

"They're just excited to have a new baby," I tell her soothingly. "Okay, too excited," I add at her steely-eyed look. "When Kashif was born—"

"When Kashif was born, you were three. Not twelve," Safiya deadpans. "Don't tell me I should give her a chance. Can we stop wasting time talking about this now? Ever since the baby was born, there's only been one thing in my life that hasn't changed. Me and you. I want this to be a summer to remember. No school, no wailing babies, no drama. Please. I literally don't want to deal with anyone else's problems. I have enough of my own. I can't take it."

I try to smile and appear enthusiastic. "Okay. I promise we will never bring up N—the baby when we're together. I know I've been busy with the store, but we're going to do everything on your list this summer and it's going to be awesome. Starting tomorrow." Amma closes the store on Wednesdays, so it's perfect. "Which of the things on your list do you want to do first? What do you say we go swimming?"

"Yes, pool day!" Safiya perks up and I sigh in relief. "By the way, I heard what you said about the waistcoat, and Ainy Zain, you can do better than that."

"Wow, thanks for the vote of confidence," I laugh. "I thought you believed in me. And I was being serious about the waist . . ."

The rest of my words shrivel up in my throat when a teenage girl walks into the store with a bag slung over one shoulder. She's got dark brown hair pulled back into an effortless half ponytail and she's dressed in black jeans and a black T-shirt that says AROMA in fancy lettering across the front.

Beside me, I hear Safiya suck in a huge breath. Her expression flips from confusion to realization to shock, and then it finally clicks with me what I'm seeing. Who I'm looking at.

It's Bajjo. My sister isn't wearing her hijab.

"Hey, guys," Bajjo says, looking down at the floor.

For a moment, it feels as if time stops. I'm so alarmed that all I can do is stare. No, there has to be some kind of mistake. Bajjo must've taken her hijab off to fix her hair, or maybe the one she wears to work at the café is different and she was in the middle of switching when she got here—

But I don't see her carrying a scarf anywhere.

My eyes dart around frantically like they're searching for something—anything—to shield Bajjo from view. Because there's no way she forgot her hijab on *purpose*.

A feeling like a sudden fever takes over me, making my stomach sink. I open my mouth, but Bajjo breezes past us to the back room and disappears. All Safiya and I can do is blink at each other, stunned.

"Did you see that? You saw that, right?" Safiya whispers.

Wordlessly, I spring out of my chair and Safiya follows me to where Bajjo is stashing her bag on one of the shelves.

"Salaam, beta," says Amma. "How was your shift earlier?"

Bajjo offers an exaggerated shrug. "Fine. The tips are good." Her voice is tense. I look between Amma and Bajjo for any clue as to what's happening. But nothing out of the ordinary might as well be happening for all the attention Amma's paying her. The bad feeling inside me grows. Has Amma even noticed what's different about Bajjo?

Bajjo fiddles with her sleeve, her gaze flitting up to me and Safiya shyly and back down again. This is not my sister. This is a stranger in my sister's skin. I don't know why, but it makes me mad. Mad because I don't *get* it. There has to be a logical explanation for this. Part of me wants to know what happened between last night and today, but another part of me is afraid to find out the answer. What on earth would make my sister give up a part of herself that she's always been so proud of?

Finally, I find the guts to speak. "Is there something you want to tell us?"

"No," Bajjo retorts. The lump in my throat grows.

"You better be joking," I say.

"Well, I'm not." Bajjo's lips are pressed into a razor-sharp line.

Safiya bites her thumbnail, looking like she's on the

verge of making a run for it. Amma watches me and Bajjo warily, like she can't understand why we're fighting right now. Well, how did she expect me to react? No one warned me!

Before I can string together any one of the millions of thoughts racing through my head, a high-pitched *ding!* from the bell out front rends the taut air.

"Hello? Is anybody here?"

A customer. Amma adjusts her niqab and stands immediately to assist them. Bajjo scurries after Amma like she's her plate of armor. I breathe in through my nose before going out to face the customer, but wind up choking on my own spit when I see who's standing out front.

Gabina Auntie.

Ugh, where's the stop button on this lousy day? Gabina Auntie's never ordered anything from Naseerah's Almari before, much less stepped foot inside the store. I didn't think we were up to her "standards."

Amma appears taken aback, too, but she puts on her professional voice. "Salaam, Gabina. What brings you in today?"

Gabina Auntie's beady eyes land on Bajjo. Her eyebrows cinch together questioningly, a frown carving her mouth like she ate something distasteful. Amma notices her staring too closely at Bajjo and diverts Gabina Auntie's eyes back to her by repeating her question.

"Right," Gabina Auntie drawls. She smooths the front of her hijab and adjusts the straps of her Louis Vuitton purse. She doesn't even bother with small talk, just launches right into an explanation. "My niece is getting married at the end of the summer. Quite unexpectedly." She sounds exasperated. "She's chosen eight of her closest friends as her bridesmaids and she wants them to wear custom matching dresses. I was wondering if you'd be able to make them. It would be a rush order."

"When would the dresses need to be ready by?" asks Amma.

"First week of August," Gabina Auntie says. "I've asked a few places, but no one can guarantee that time-line." Yeah, no wonder. That's only seven weeks away. It would be a huge hassle. "Ambreen advised me to ask you. My niece looked up your work online and she has a few acquaintances who've ordered from you in the past, and they've all had nothing but good things to say. We'll pay double if that's what it takes to meet the deadline."

Bajjo and I share a quick glance and I know we're both thinking about the tracker. That's a big order. Amma already has her hands full. There's no way she can do all that in such a short amount of time.

But . . . it's also a lot of money.

Amma goes over to her computer and pulls up a blank customer order form to start filling it out. "Does your niece have a favorite design in mind?"

"I can send you a couple of examples," Gabina Auntie clucks. "It needs to be modest and one of a kind. Sounds right up your alley, Naseerah. I'm sure you'll knock it out of the park."

Amma nods and I can't tell if she's smiling or not. Once she's done typing out all the information, she prints out the form along with a price quote and hands them to Gabina Auntie. "If all this looks good, you can sign on the dotted line and I will get to work on these right away."

CHAPTER 9

"Seven weeks. Eight outfits. For *Gabina* Auntie?" I enunciate to my reflection in the community pool. "Amma's lost her mind." Bajjo thinks so, too. She won't say it out loud, but I know. Then again, Bajjo hasn't been saying a whole lot of anything to me since the bombshell she dropped yesterday.

Safiya pops her sport-hijab-covered head out of the water and pushes her goggles up onto her head. I'm not that great of a swimmer, so I stick to the pool's edge. "Ainy, not to sound mean, but you've already said that, like, five times since we got here. If you think making the dresses for Gabina Auntie's niece is bad news, then just tell your mom that."

But that's just it. It's not bad news. In fact, it's worth it for Amma if it means her work will get a lot of exposure through Yasir's mom's connections. It could bring even more business for Amma, and then maybe Bajjo can leave her other job and come back to Naseerah's Almari full-time. I wonder if Amma was thinking about Abu and Dadi when she accepted the near-impossible project. Bajjo's already working another job to cover that, but maybe it's still not enough. Seriously, why do we need so much money to live in the world? My parents always say that our rizq—sustenance—comes from Allah, but it would be nice to have some money, too. Why did it have to be so unfair sometimes? Awful people like Yasir's family get to live in huge houses and drive fancy cars; meanwhile, my family can't even afford to have our own place to live.

I hug my arms around my body, watching Safiya bob up and down in the water. The hot afternoon sun brought almost the entire neighborhood out today. Little kids are splashing around in the kiddie pool. Adults are lounging in the shade or reading on the deck. A group of teenagers are racing each other at the deeper end like they're competing in the Olympics.

Safiya grabs hold of the side of the pool and flips onto her back with her arms and legs straight out. "So, have you talked to your sister about, you know?" she asks the sky.

"No," I snort, but the question stings.

I know a lot of Muslim girls stop wearing hijab for different reasons, but I never thought my sister would be one of them! She has always been my role model and the main reason why I wanted to be a hijabi. One of the things I love about my sister is that she doesn't let the haters bother her. Bajjo standing her ground always made me wish my confidence would hurry up and show its face so that I could start wearing it, too. Her taking it off feels like she betrayed *me*. It feels like she did it to sway me out of putting it on. I know it's a ridiculous assumption, but I can't help it. And I don't know what else to think, since Bajjo still refuses to explain why she took her hijab off no matter how many times I ask her about it.

If Bajjo can't even confide in me anymore, then can I honestly tell her about the whole Yasir mess? Would she even listen, or care?

And I know I can't tell Amma now. She's already got enough problems to deal with. She doesn't even have time to give me design lessons, much less fix my silly boy problems. The same boy whose mom gave *my* mom her biggest sale yet. I can't mess things up for Amma's business by starting something between our families. We might as well return Gabina Auntie's deposit.

Safiya plunges in and out of the water in front of me. She looks peaceful, like she's in her element. Or maybe it's because we're finally doing something just for us. I could tell Safiya about Yasir's messages. Crush or no crush, she wouldn't find them very funny. But Safiya told me yesterday she didn't want to talk about Noor or deal with anyone else's problems. I don't want to be a downer and take away these few hours of joy from her either by ruining our day off together talking about Yasir. She already sounded kind of annoyed when I kept bringing up work just now.

Ugh, when did I become so boring? I'm probably overreacting. I should just handle Yasir on my own. Yeah, that's it. Next time I bump into him, I'm going to make it extra clear he needs to move on. End of story.

"Earth to Ainy!" A curtain of sun-warmed water explodes in my face and I cough, scrubbing chlorine out of my eyes to huff at Safiya. "Good, I thought you fell asleep. Let's have a race! Loser has to give up their half of the extra-cheesy fries to the winner!"

I gasp. I will never, ever surrender my extra-cheesy

fries, especially not the ones from the popular burger joint Safiya's mom's taking us to for lunch.

"You're on!" We both swim to a side of the pool that's not as crowded so our paths aren't blocked by bodies.

"On your mark," Safiya intones, lowering her goggles back onto her face. "Get set. Go!"

I inhale a huge gulp of oxygen before pushing off the wall. Beside me, Safiya shoots forward, pumping her arms. Between the two of us, it's obvious who took swimming lessons as a kid. I wade clumsily and resort to running, pushing forward as fast as I can. Safiya looks over her shoulder and cracks up because I probably resemble a drowning zombie.

"Just quit now, Zain! Mmm, I can already smell the—"

"For the cheesy fries!" I cry out, and even *I'm* surprised when I close the distance between us with a giant leap. Safiya doesn't even have time to scream before I catch her around the neck and drag us both underwater. We both resurface at the same time, coughing and breathing hard.

Safiya slaps my arm at my wacky grin. "Cheater. You suck."

I level a serious look in her direction. "The stakes were high. I did what I had to."

Safiya tries to hold on to a scowl and fails. She bursts out laughing. A few seconds later, I join her, my heart ballooning with delight for the first time in days. It feels amazing to forget everything else going on in my life for one teensy tiny little moment.

"Bombs away!" The loud voice and thumping footsteps on the pool deck are the only noises that alert us before four blurs jump into the pool around us like cannonballs. *Splash! Splash! Splash! Splash!* One after the other. When heads start bobbing above the water, all my mirth evaporates. And despite the sunny afternoon, my whole body goes cold.

"Who invited them?" Safiya hisses when Yasir, Mustafa, Abdul, and Shezi flash us rogue grins, shaking their heads and scattering water droplets across our faces like overly happy dogs. They clasp hands and form a circle around me and Safiya, hooting and hollering while they spin in some bizarre imitation of ring-around-the-rosy. I shrink back like they're a pack of sharks. Safiya snags my elbow and hugs me close to her side.

"Didn't know this was a zoo," she mumbles so that only I can hear. "Hey, losers! Scram!" Safiya screams over their trilling voices. "We were here first."

"This is a public pool," Mustafa states. He drifts past us, doing slow backstrokes. "And it's in *our* neighborhood. Not yours."

A vein throbs in Safiya's forehead. Yasir pushes his wet hair back from his forehead and winks at me. I look away, heat zipping through me. The only skin I'm showing is my face, hands, and feet, and yet suddenly I feel completely exposed. To top it off, my swimsuit isn't very cute, but good-quality modest swimwear is expensive, man.

Safiya looks ready to violently throw them out of the pool with her bare hands, but she stops dead in her tracks and the color drains from her face. "Oh no. I have to go."

"What?" Now I'm panicking. "Why?"

Safiya spews the word *period* and catapults out of the pool, running to the changing rooms as fast as her legs can carry her.

"Yo, where's the fire?" Abdul snickers, cramming his head too close to mine for comfort. I swing sideways to insert space between us. I should get out of the pool, too, but Safiya was right. We were here first! She and I shouldn't have to leave because the boys showed up and made things awkward.

Speaking of awkward . . . Yasir's only a few feet away. It's now or never. There's really no good way to break it to him. I just wish I didn't have to do this while we're both soaking and one of us is shirtless.

I straighten my spine and wade over to Yasir, floating at a safe distance. "Hey, can I talk to you? Over there."

Yasir's face splits into a gigantic grin and I really hate that it makes him look more like Izyaan. "Sure, Ainy. Be right back, guys!" The others break into a chorus of *wooo*s and kissy sounds. Disgusting. I bet Yasir even gives them a thumbs-up. I wouldn't know. I don't turn to look at him until we're standing on top of the submerged steps. I suck down my unease and force a smile, but keep it tame so as not to look too friendly.

"Look, I, uh, think you're nice and all that, but I don't . . ." A bead of sweat slides down my face, mixing with the pool water already there. *You don't feel the same way! Just say it, Ainy!*

Yasir's lips flatten at my shaky voice. "You don't what? *Like* me like me?" he asks.

"No. I mean, yes! Wait, that's not what I—"

"That's not fair, Ainy. You didn't even give me a chance to prove myself."

Am I supposed to do that first? All I know is I don't want to. But I don't know how to explain that to Yasir without upsetting him even more than he already is. He's waiting for an explanation, but my brain is fidgeting, unable to come up with a single good excuse, and I can feel the others silently communicating behind our backs and—

"I like Izyaan," I say. Both my and Yasir's eyes blow up into two moons at the same time. Bile climbs up my throat. I can't believe I just admitted that out loud! To Yasir! The pressure of being put on the spot made me do it! It's too late now. There's no taking it back. I might as well roll with it and hope it'll at least put Yasir off.

"It's true. I'm into Izyaan." Each word feels like glass scraping up my throat. *Stop it, Ainy! Before you make it worse.* "So. Yeah."

Yasir is so still he could pass for one of Amma's mannequins. He stares at me sharply, like he's trying to see right through me. Finally, he scoffs, "Whatever you say, Ainy," before pivoting and swimming back to his friends. His hands slap the water way too hard, the sound ricocheting against my eardrums.

Before he's even made it back to Abdul, Shezi, and Mustafa, I pick myself up and flee from the pool, nearly wiping out on the deck and spraining my ankle in the process.

Oh my God, what have I done? Now Izyaan's for sure

going to find out that I have a crush on him! What if he thinks I'm weird—or even worse, he's grossed out—and never talks to me again?

But the scariest thought that comes to mind is: If any of the parents find out, I'm so going to get it.

CHAPTER 10

It's Friday night. Guess where I am? At home. Sporting my ugliest pajamas and watching my favorite Muslim couple's latest vlog instead of at the movies with Safiya. Like we were supposed to be. I bailed on her last minute, faking a cold.

AINY HOW COULD YOU DO THIS TO ME? Safiya mourned over text.

I replied, I knoww I'm rly sorry :(it came out of nowhere.

Safiya: Kk, feel better! let me know if you need anything.

I don't tell Safiya the truth. That I'm too embarrassed to leave the house in case I run into Izyaan on the way in or out. That aside from bolting to Naseerah's Almari to work, I haven't left the house since me and my big mouth goofed up at the pool on Wednesday. At this point, I bet Yasir's already gone and blabbed to Izyaan about how I'm in love with him. I would rather wear the same pair of underwear for the rest of my life than show my face to Izyaan ever again.

Not to mention the Khalids are having a dawat—a party, a get-together, whatever you want to call it—tonight. Muffled footsteps and chatter seep through the floorboards. Outside in the backyard, the uncles are on the deck grilling and talking super loudly. No way was I going to risk being seen going out. I'd get roped into sticking around. We were invited, of course, but I was majorly relieved when Amma excused herself to catch up on orders. Bajjo was scheduled to close at Aroma and she dropped Kashif off at the masjid to play basketball with Sheikh Samiullah and some other boys his age. Even my little brother has more of a life than me. He's not the loser scarfing down leftover pizza in front of Bajjo's laptop on a summer weekend.

"Where are my scissors?" I hear Amma complain to herself from the living room. "Ainy! Did you take them?"

"From all the way over here?" I answer around a mouthful of pizza.

"I know I put them down right—ah! Never mind. Found them."

I pause With Love, Leena's try-on haul video to go see if Amma could use an extra set of hands and *holy cow!* Okay, it's not totally weird for our place to be untidy, but this is some other level of chaos. It looks like a clearance rack threw up in here. No wonder Amma couldn't find her scissors. Clothes are covering every square inch of floor and furniture. Garment bags and plastic bags full of them. I have to play the floor is lava to reach Amma hunched over on the rug in the living room, fitting sleeves onto a blue sari blouse.

"Call the authorities." I yak. "This is a crime scene!"

Amma squints up at me with puffy eyes like she can't figure out how I got there. Her skin looks kind of dull and dry, too.

"Amma," I say, worried. "Are you okay?"

She sets the blouse and needle down, stretching her neck to rest her head on the sofa behind her. "I think"— she sighs, sounding defeated—"I've bitten off more than I can chew."

"Uh, what do you mean?" I ask.

"I mean, I can't keep up." Amma blows a loose strand of hair out of her eyes. "I think it's time I put a pause on taking new orders until I'm caught up. At least until I'm done with Gabina's bridesmaid dresses. I haven't even gotten a chance to start on those yet. There are several other orders on my list I need to do first."

I look around at the dozens of orders piled up around the Khalids' basement. "But . . . aren't we going to lose money if we stop taking work?"

Amma sops air into both cheeks and exhales slowly. "I'll figure something out. It wouldn't be the best business decision to pause orders just as I'm establishing myself at the new place." Amma sighs, considering her hands. "But Gabina's is a big project, Ainy. That one alone can cover a whole month's worth of bills. I can't say no to that." Amma also hates letting people down, especially brides. She was already a goner when Gabina Auntie told her no one else could do the job.

And then I'm struck by the perfect idea.

"I'll do it," I volunteer. "I'll design the bridesmaid dresses and you can keep working on everything else."

"Ainy—"

"Bajjo told me she's working at Aroma because we need the money." I didn't mean to blurt it out like that, but I figured it would get Amma's attention. I was right. Her face crumples and for the first time in my life, Amma looks . . . old to me.

She buries her face in her hands. "You weren't supposed to know that," Amma says softly. "I already feel horrible about Kulsoom pitching in. She's sixteen. She should be spending that money on herself or saving it for college, not—" Amma can't go on. Tears glimmer in her brown eyes and my heart cracks down the middle, but now I'm determined. I meant what I said to Abu. I want to help. And now I finally have the chance by doing what I wanted all along. Designing clothes is the only thing I *can* do. That way, I'll feel like I'm doing something.

"Please, Amma. Let me design the dresses," I say, kneeling beside her. "I know I can do it. I *want* to do it. I follow a bunch of Muslim lifestyle and beauty influencers. I know what's in." Amma's specialty is desi clothes—not that she isn't talented in other areas, too, but I'm trying to build my case here. "I promise I'll work really hard. They'll be the best thing ever. You'll see. Just give me a chance."

Amma folds her arms across her chest, her head swiveling this way and that, like she's trying to find a way out of a maze she got lost in. At some point, she must realize

I'm the key, like one of those power-ups in Kashif's video games that give his player an extra boost to win.

"All right," she agrees reluctantly. "On two conditions. You don't fall behind on your other duties at the store. That always comes first. And I want to see how the idea is coming along every step of the way. I'm going to need at least two weeks to make the dresses, so we need to finalize a design enough in advance to ensure I can get all the materials on time. Think four weeks is enough for you?"

I squeal and roll into a mound of plastic bags with my arms over my head. "YESSS!" Four weeks is plenty of time. This is going to be a piece of cake!

"Quratulain, shhhh! They have guests upstairs," Amma reminds me, but my elated reaction has brought a smile to her face.

It feels like sunbeams are shining out of every single one of my pores. In this moment, nothing can bring me down—not cancer, not Bajjo, not even Yasir.

"Oh, speaking of upstairs," Amma says, cutting my celebration short. "Ambreen keeps texting me. She's really insisting we join the party for a little bit. I feel bad turning her down so many times. Why don't you and I swing by for ten minutes? I could use a break and it'll make Ambreen happy."

I freeze mid-roll, my giddiness morphing into instant panic. "But I'm in my pajamas," I blurt.

Amma looks at me funny. "So am I. Let's both get changed and meet in front of the stairs in five minutes."

In my room, my anxiety skyrockets. Normally, I would take my time picking out the right outfit, but all I can focus on is coming up with an excuse to get out of going upstairs. What do I tell Amma? *Sorry, I can't go because there's a high chance Izyaan knows I have a crush on him, and I'd rather combust than face him.*

Amma is already in a pretty blue abaya and niqab when I emerge wearing a plain green-and-black shalwar kameez. It's not the first thing I would've picked if I'd been thinking straight, but I have a bigger problem on my hands.

It's fine, Ainy, I tell myself as Amma and I climb the basement stairs to the house's main level. Izyaan's probably hanging out in his room with the boys. I might not even see him. I'll hang out for a few minutes to be polite, then make my escape.

Amma knocks on the basement door before cracking it open. To the left is the Khalids' kitchen and to the right is the family room where all the aunties are gathered, chatting it up with their plates of food. Sister Ambreen stops mid-conversation when she catches sight of us and stands up, grinning. "Naseerah! Ainy! I'm so happy you came."

Amma goes over to greet the fancy-dressed women. It's a mixture of the Khalids' family and friends. We know most of them, including—

"Salaam, Naseerah," Gabina Auntie says, leaning in for a stiff hug.

Yasir's here. Now I really want to throw up.

After the aunties are done patting my head and commenting on how quickly I'm growing up, Sister Ambreen steers me and Amma toward the kitchen and the buffet spread out on the counter. "Please, don't be shy," Sister Ambreen says, stuffing plates into our hands. "Take as much as you like. There's plenty of food. Ainy, the girls are upstairs in Amarah's room."

You mean upstairs where there's a greater chance I could run into Izyaan? I'll pass. I don't know what to say out loud, so I just smile and nod. Amma takes her food back to the family room while I stir the tray of nihari, stalling. How long before the adults notice I'm still here? Maybe if I'm quick, I can safely make it to Amarah's room without the boys seeing me.

Gripping my plate, I head for the staircase right

outside the kitchen and break into a sprint. I'm halfway up when I hear them.

"I hope there's biryani left."

"You mean you didn't eat the whole tray already?"

The hair on the back of my neck stands up. *Shoot!* I stop dead in my tracks, almost dropping my plate. In a flash, I turn around and make a beeline back the other way. I leap to hide behind the fake tree next to the staircase. Except I'm not winning an award for world's greatest sleuth, because Cocoa the cat chooses that exact moment to scurry past me. I trip over him, crashing into the tree and knocking it over. I yell out as I pitch forward, nihari splattering all over the floor. The whole house suddenly falls silent at the sound of my embarrassing fall. Things turn ten times worse when I look up and find Yasir and Izyaan staring at me sprawled on top of the tree like I fell out of the sky.

"Ainy?" Izyaan asks.

I stand quickly, smoothing down my clothes and fixing my headband.

"H-hi," I stammer with my cheeks on fire. "Sorry. Wasn't looking." *Please kill me now.*

Just then, Amma and Sister Ambreen round the corner

to see what all the ruckus is. Amma gasps at the mess and the greasy nihari stains on my kameez. "What happened?"

This is so humiliating.

"It was an accident," Izyaan says as Sister Ambreen goes to grab cleaning supplies. Meanwhile, Izyaan leans down and lifts the tree back into place. Yasir shoots his cousin dagger eyes like Izyaan got down on one knee and asked me to marry him. Amma takes the paper towels and cleaning spray from Sister Ambreen when she returns and passes them to me with a stern look.

"Ainy will take care of it," Amma says before Sister Ambreen can object, and leads her back to the family room while apologizing repeatedly on my behalf.

I get on my hands and knees and start wiping the hardwood floors and bits of fake mulch that fell out of the planter. I'm even more mortified when Izyaan bends down to give me a hand.

"You don't have to," I mumble. Especially not when I currently reek of beef stew.

Izyaan shrugs. "It's no big deal. It'll get done faster if we work together."

He's acting like nothing's off. That can't be right. You want me to believe Yasir *didn't* tell Izyaan that I have a humongous crush on him, and Izyaan isn't going to make it clear to me that *ew, gross, I don't like you like that, Ainy; don't ever talk to me again?* Maybe he wants to, but now he's chickening out. Maybe he doesn't want to be mean and call me out when I've already made a scene in front of everyone. Or maybe—

He doesn't know. Izyaan is being his normal, friendly self. Behind him, Yasir just stands there like he's too good to help clean up. He considers us like he's waiting for something to happen, but I don't know what. There's something in the air I'm not quite putting together. But one thing's for sure: Yasir didn't tell Izyaan my secret. Why not? That doesn't make any sense! It's the perfect way for Yasir to get back at me for shutting him down at the pool.

Yasir drives his toes into Izyaan's back and says irately, "C'mon, Iz. The others are waiting for us."

"We made them pause our game while we got more food," Izyaan clarifies to me, even though I didn't ask. Yasir seems angry, like he's ready to kick Izyaan if he doesn't move it ASAP. Wow, he really wants to get away from me today. That's a welcome change.

Then it clicks. No, wait. Not him. Yasir wants *Izyaan* to get away from me. Of course! Yasir isn't telling Izyaan about my crush on purpose, because he's afraid *Izyaan might like me back*. If Izyaan stays oblivious, then Yasir thinks he still has a shot with me.

My insides wilt. If Yasir knowing that I like Izyaan isn't even good enough for him to lose interest, then what is? I'm back at square one. What the heck do I do now?

CHAPTER 11

I'm so excited about breaking the news to Bajjo that I completely forget she's avoiding me and ambush her when she comes into the store the next day. "Bajjo, guess what? Amma's letting me design the bridesmaid dresses for Gabina Auntie's niece!"

To my surprise, she actually smiles at me like how the old Bajjo used to. "Wow, Ainy. That's great! I'm really happy for you."

I hop on one foot like a hyper bunny rabbit, desperate to keep Bajjo talking as long as she's in a good mood, but I stop short when I notice Amarah right behind her. She's hoisting a backpack and a Frappuccino in one hand.

"Salaam, Ainy!" Amarah waves at me cheerfully with her free hand. Too bad I'm not as happy to see her. "It feels like I haven't talked to you in a long time. You should come upstairs and hang out sometimes. Hold the nihari." Amarah snickers into her straw. Super. I'm never going to hear the end of that one.

"No, thanks. I'm busy," I say. And it probably comes out ruder than I intended because Bajjo shoots me a warning glance. Just like that, the old Bajjo is gone again.

If Amarah noticed my tone, she ignores it. "Oh, I believe you," she says. "The invitation still stands, though." I almost wish she wasn't so nice. No surprise there, I guess. It's a family trait.

"Amarah's staying until we close shop," Bajjo declares. The two older girls walk around me to set their stuff down and my annoyance spikes at Amarah claiming Safiya's usual spot behind the counter with her laptop. Steam builds up inside my ears, but I tell myself to chill out. Safiya's always here, and Amma never complains. Bajjo's allowed to have her friend over, too. Except I work here way more than Bajjo now. She's at Aroma every morning, then arrives at Naseerah's Almari after more than half the day is up, which is when I get to take a break.

"'Kay, I'm gonna go now," I say. "Safiya and I are going shopping."

"Have fun!" Amarah chirps. "There are some awesome Fourth of July sales going on."

Bajjo doesn't offer any advice. She takes up the computer mouse and starts telling Amarah a funny story about one of her Aroma coworkers mixing up two people's orders today. Bajjo's hair is casually braided down one shoulder. It's her favorite way to style it. I'm still not used to seeing her look like this except at home. It looks all wrong.

Amarah still wears her headscarf as naturally as putting shoes on to leave the house. Does she know what happened to change Bajjo's mind about the hijab? If it were me, Safiya would definitely know. If Amarah does know the whole story, she's not giving anything away. Everything is normal between Bajjo and Amarah.

I head out without saying goodbye, feeling like I got pushed out of the room.

"You're going to be famous," says Safiya when I tell her the news. "Do you know the kind of people Gabina Auntie's friends with?" Safiya fans her fingers wide like she's demonstrating a burst of stars. "My mom says they're all a big deal. Doctors, business owners, Pakistani military families. You name it."

We weren't really hungry, so we grabbed bubble tea instead. I blow nervously into my straw, making my milk tea gurgle as Safiya and I browse a sales rack at one of the town center's boutiques. "Gee, thanks, Safiya. Way to take the pressure off."

"You're welcome. Have you started working on the design yet?"

"Not yet. I promised Amma I'd watch the front desk first," I respond. "What do you think of this?" I dig out a green ruffle-trim smock dress with long sleeves. Don't get me wrong—I hate it. But summer's a tough time to find modest clothes. Everything's low-necked, cropped, or sleeveless. I'll wear something under or over if I have to, but I don't like it unless it's part of the look.

Safiya wrinkles her nose like the dress stinks. "For real, Ainy? I'm not letting you wear that in public. What gives, anyway? That's the fourth thing you've shown me that's not you."

"What do you mean?"

"I mean, they're not your style. The Ainy I know has glitz," Safiya says, gesturing at what I'm currently wearing.

It's a purple silk blouse with tight-fit lace sleeve cuffs and a cute bow at the neck that matches the little bows catching the light on my flats.

I sigh. It's so much easier to order my clothes online, where I have tons of better modest options, but I can never afford what I want on my measly budget even when I use content creator discount codes. Safiya's family is having so many parties coming up I want to dress up for! There's Noor's aqeeqah in August. The Messaoudis also celebrate the Fourth of July, Algeria's Independence Day on July fifth, and Pakistan's Independence Day on August fourteenth. And since they didn't go to Algeria this year, Safiya's dad's side of the family invited me over to their house on July fifth for the first time in forever. Every year, Safiya's jiddati—grandmother—makes shakshouka and couscous, and then she tells stories remembering the shaheed—the martyrs—who died in the war for independence from the French.

"Let's check out someplace else," I say, putting the rejected green dress back.

"I actually have to go now," Safiya says glumly, glancing down at her phone. "My mom and khala are waiting for me at Sephora. I didn't find anything I like either. We'll try again later." Safiya slurps the rest of her bubble tea until all that's left is air. Then she hugs me and skips off, promising to text me later.

I have a few minutes of my break left, so I roam around the town center. The less time I have to spend third wheeling Bajjo and Amarah, the happier I'll be. I don't go too far, though. Amma doesn't let me go past the commercial zone into the residential area by myself. Fine by me. Maybe in the next five minutes, I'll luck out and find something that looks good, is cheap, and actually covers my butt.

A girl can dream, right?

CHAPTER 12

On Wednesday, Safiya wants to come over and have a baking contest with Kashif, but I need to use my day off to concentrate on the bridesmaid dresses. Amma gave me the assignment five days ago and all I have are basic outlines that I managed to scrawl in my downtime at the store. So much for being bored. I swear we've gotten even busier in the last couple of days.

But now I'm kicking it into high gear. I promise Safiya that I'm almost done and we can have all the fun once I'm off the hook. Then I grab a juice box from the fridge, stake my claim at the dining table, and get down to business. Kashif's building a five-hundred-piece puzzle of the solar system across from me. I tune out his voice as he mumbles to himself and try to get in the zone to do my thing.

Most fashion designers who want to make it big envision their clothes being modeled on runways. But one of the first things Amma ever taught me was to think about the subject first and foremost. *Think about who is going to be wearing it*, she said. *What would be the perfect fit?* Amma's like a librarian, but instead of matching books to readers, she matches clothes to people.

I'm putting the finishing touches on two possible designs that I can't wait to show Amma. One is simple satin and drops straight down. It has this one-shoulder bell sleeve shape to it on top, but of course, full sleeves on both sides. I added a rhinestone waist belt to give it a splash of elegance. I'm thinking it needs to be mint green. You can't go wrong with mint colors, especially for bridesmaids.

The second one is the opposite and, okay, I admit I went a *tad* bit overboard with it, but I love it. Everyone has a way of expressing their personal style. Some people like neutrals and black all day every day. Others—like yours truly—like big bold colors and heavy craftsmanship. This other dress design is princess ball gown meets enchanted fairy garden. There are lace bows shaped like actual wings, and the multicolor skirts poof out like flower petals. Basically, the stuff dreams are made of.

"Do you want mac 'n' cheese?" Kashif asks.

"Not hungry," I reply absently.

Kashif turns his head to the side. "What're you scribbling?"

"They are not scribbles! I'm designing dresses for Amma," I reply with an air of importance.

Kashif screws up his face like he doesn't believe me. "They look like hot-air balloons."

I point my pencil's eraser at him. "I know what I'm doing. Finish your puzzle."

"Amma's gonna think they're ugly," Kashif sings.

"What do you know about designing?" I snap. An hour later, I put the finishing touches on the sketches, smearing graphite all over the side of my hand, and slap my pencil down on the table. "I got this. Watch."

I saunter past Kashif and into Amma's room. She's sitting on her bed reading Qur'an. I really shouldn't interrupt her, but I'm excited and impatient.

I hold up the drawings in both my hands in a big reveal. "Ta-da!"

Amma scrunches up her eyebrows. "What's this?"

"The designs for Gabina Auntie." Okay, maybe Kashif wasn't exaggerating about the hot-air balloon comparison. I suck at drawing. The ideas inside my head always look fantastic, but I can never make them look as good in real life. I know the concepts are great, though, so I explain to Amma out loud, using my pencil as a guide.

My smile starts to fade when Amma doesn't react as I suspected. She isn't beaming at me like I'm a genius or nodding her head like she can't decide which one of my designs is better because she thinks both are brilliant. She's just thoughtfully quiet.

When I'm done with my spiel, Amma takes both of the drawings from me and lays them down side by side on her pillow. "I like your directions. But this one is a bit overdone," she says gently, pointing at the bell sleeve dress design. "We need a more original concept. And this other one is beautiful and ethereal, but I'm not sure that it's right for the occasion. We don't want the bridesmaids to out-shine the bride, you know?" My spirit deflates. I thought the fairy princess dress was a sure winner. Suddenly, I feel very small.

Amma lays a hand on my shoulder reassuringly. "I can tell you worked hard on these, Ainy, and I know it's dis-couraging when something you put your whole heart into is turned down. But that's the nature of art. I'm not saying they aren't good enough. I'm saying they aren't a fit for the project. I've had lots of clients who don't like my design on the first or second or even third pass. The key is to keep trying until you find the right one."

My mouth falls open. I always assumed Amma's customers loved everything she made for them on the first try! "But how do you know what's the right one?" I ask.

Amma smiles. "When you do this for as long as I have, you learn to read the words people aren't saying out loud. Trust your instincts."

I pull a confused face. Gabina Auntie didn't really give us detailed instructions. All she sent us were pictures of a couple of popular styles and said the dresses needed to be one of a kind. How does that make any sense? But even if I do manage to come up with an out-of-this-world idea, who knows if Gabina Auntie will agree. She could make us do the design all over again if she doesn't like it. My head spins. This whole thing just got bigger and more complicated.

"Try again, Ainy," Amma says, squeezing my hand. "I know you can do this. You have time."

Kashif looks up from the two puzzle pieces he's trying to force together when I return to the table. He takes one look at my face and says, "Told you."

I sigh. My failed drawings flutter to the floor as I

face-plant on the table. "I'll have some of that mac 'n' cheese now."

Twenty minutes later, I'm sulking in my room, but at least I have a steaming bowl of Kashif's creamy baked mac 'n' cheese to cheer me up. Even though Amma let me down easy, it still feels like I got flattened inside a textbook. A math textbook because it hurts extra hard. I'm so disappointed in myself. *Fairy garden dress.* Please, what was I thinking? It was a stupid idea. I can't believe I thought Amma would instantly fall in love with it. This just proves I'm an amateur designer.

I jut my chin out. I have to keep trying. Besides, our deadline is still more than seven weeks away. That's plenty of time for me to come up with the perfect design and for Amma to make the dresses. And I think I know where to find the inspiration I need.

I whip out my phone, tap open a few apps, and start digging through hashtags like #MuslimFashion, #ModestClothing, #ModestFashion, and #Bridesmaids. Just as I suspected, some of my favorite Muslim influencer accounts pop up. If anyone is going to have a feel for what's in, it's gotta be the people who get brand deals and have thousands of followers, right?

My eyes widen like saucers when I see the number of posts. And the more I scroll, the more pages load with drop-dead gorgeous outfits that make me want to reach through my screen and steal them for myself. Princess gowns and mermaid skirts and mesh panel dresses in dazzling colors. I start writing down a list of things I keep seeing over and over again—the popular stuff that everyone's trying to copy. I let out a gasp when I stumble upon a post from a Muslim fashion brand a few days ago with a hijabi model sporting a floor-length beige dress. It has bishop sleeves, a pleated skirt, and shiny golden buttons down one side of the coat-like bodice. It's both sophisticated and light and yup, I'm head over heels. I immediately save the post. My brain's already firing up with different variations for the bridesmaid dresses when I suddenly spot the top comment underneath the post.

I'm sorry, but this is hideous. Who actually wants to wear something like this?

My fingers freeze over my phone screen. The comment has hundreds of likes. There are people who are arguing with the original commenter, but there are a lot *taking* her side, too.

Seriously, I don't understand this modest "fashion" trend. It's not fashion. It's boring.

I feel bad for Muslim girls. They don't get to dress up properly. What's the point when you have to walk around in so many layers? Don't they get hot and itchy?

Blood froths loudly in my ears, but I can't stop. I can't look away. Hideous? Boring? Not *real* fashion? Says *who?*

Sorry, you can't convince me the hijab is sexy no matter how hard you try.

That last one has a reply under it that stops me in my tracks.

I'm Muslim, and I agree with you. There's no point in hijab if you're still going to wear things that are going to draw attention to yourself.

Okay, I'm no stranger to reading negative comments online, especially under modest fashion and hijabi accounts, but what do these people have against modest clothes, anyway? They really think the way Muslim women dress—the way I dress—is *that* ugly? That it's not fashionable? No one's making them wear it if they don't want to! I've never thought that the way Amma or Bajjo or Safiya or Muslim influencers got ready is ugly. Not once. And no one is trying to make hijab look sexy!! That's literally not the point. On top of that, this random woman is saying we aren't allowed to look or feel beautiful even with hijab on? How come Amma has so many clients, then?

My head droops and I stare at the beige dress that took less than five seconds for me to fall in love with. I still can't see anything wrong with it. But what do I know? Maybe *I'm* wrong. If so many people agree with the comment, then there must be something that I'm missing. Besides, I know now I'm not a good designer. Amma sort of told me as much. I still have so much to learn.

What's the point in becoming a hijab-wearing fashion designer if people are going to think that I, the designer, am never fashionable? Wearing hijab automatically means I'm not qualified to create beautiful things, and it also means I'm not allowed to be stylish because that would make me stand out?

Wait, is that why Yasir won't give me a break? Am I

doing something wrong by making myself stand out and sending him the wrong signals? The thought gives me a serious case of the ick. I don't want to change anything about the way I dress up! I like it.

But what if the only way to get Yasir to stop annoying me is to make myself invisible? I've always used fashion to beautify and stand out, but can the opposite be possible?

Can I use it to fade into the background?

CHAPTER 13

"Ainy! Get the phone!" Bajjo hollers at me.

"I did," I say through my teeth, cupping the phone's receiver with my hand. "*Your* phone's the one ringing! Hi? Yes, sorry. No, we, uh—can you please repeat that?" I can't understand a word the caller is yelling at me because of all the noise! Naseerah's Almari is a zoo today. I've never seen so many people in here before. It seems like everyone's got a pickup they swear Amma said would be done today or a design consultation or a complaint about their shirt's shoulder width not being right. Amma's out on the floor trying to placate the crowd.

I give up on trying to hear and hang up the phone, wincing a little at how unprofessional that was.

"How did this happen?" Bajjo hisses in my ear. She's frantically scrolling up and down in our tracker to figure out what went wrong. "Who scheduled *eleven* pickups today? You're not supposed to schedule more than six in one day! Ainy, I told you this! We never know if someone might need an alteration done on the spot after they try the clothes on. That takes even more time!"

"I . . . must not have been paying attention," I say meekly.

"Well, thanks to you, now our whole schedule's been thrown off!" I shrink back at Bajjo's blazing face. I've made mistakes at my job in the past, but nothing as big as this! I don't blame her for being so angry with me. She walked right into a mess as soon as she got here. I didn't know what was going on at first. When one customer after another started showing up nonstop, I couldn't keep up with all the questions. Amma had to come out and do damage control, and I think that's the part Bajjo's most mad about. That me screwing up has made Amma look bad.

I've just had so much on my mind lately. I didn't attend Sister Ambreen's first class on Thursday night because I was freaking out about the bridesmaid dresses. I didn't get anything done, and Safiya texted me afterward sounding extremely unhappy.

I can't believe you stood me up again!!

I've ditched her multiple times in the last couple of days and she's fed up. I know Safiya's tired of being cooped up at home and mad at me for constantly bailing on her, but I haven't been able to come up with a single new design idea to share with Amma. She asks for updates on the bridesmaid dresses, and I tell her I'm working on it, but I can tell she's getting impatient and a smidge worried. It's like my mind completely shut down after I read all those comments. Even the beige dress I was drooling over isn't doing anything to spark my imagination anymore. This has never happened to me before! It's like a switch is stuck in my head. The more I stress out about it, the more tension coils my brain and makes my mind go blank.

Amma runs around from one person to another until gradually the store starts to clear out. Unfortunately, some people are frowning. When the last person leaves, Amma closes the doors—yikes, that can't be good—and whips around to face me and Bajjo with her arms crossed.

"Who is going to tell me what happened here?" Amma asks. I've never heard her sound so distressed.

"Ask Ainy," Bajjo declares, turning to face me haughtily.

I'm on the verge of tears, but somehow manage to say, "I'm sorry. I accidentally scheduled too many pickups and didn't ask you first. It was a mistake. I wasn't thinking."

"I wish you had thought of that before, Ainy," says Amma. "I don't know if some of those people will ever come back." She sighs, wiping at her forehead with the back of her hand. "Well, what's done is done. From now on, let's promise to communicate better so it doesn't happen again."

Bajjo shakes her head and follows Amma to the back room, leaving me alone. My face is burning with shame. I shouldn't even care what Bajjo thinks because she turned on me first, but I do. I let them both down. I've never felt like such a failure. I can't design dresses for Amma to be proud of and I can't even be trusted to look after the store. Amma will probably always be looking over my shoulder now at the store like she does with my homework. Worse, she might make me stop working on the bridesmaid dresses after what happened today.

I'm a terrible friend, a terrible designer, and a terrible daughter. To top it off, I can't even lose myself in the one thing that brings me joy because I've literally lost the ability to design.

Really crying now, I take my phone and bolt from the store without telling Amma or Bajjo that I'm going on break.

———◆◆———

Crepes don't hit the same without Safiya. I thought they would cheer me up, but I feel worse sitting here by myself with tears and snot leaking down my face in the town center bookstore's café. Some kids are weaving through the shelves in the children's section and their high-pitched laughter is getting on my last nerve. Now I'm crankier than a grandma, too. This day keeps getting better and better.

"Whoa, no Safiya today? Hey, are you crying?"

I jump at the voice and quickly turn my head to dry my cheeks, but it's too late. He already saw my pathetic face, so what's the point in pretending? I'm so tired and overwhelmed I don't have the energy to put up much of a fight. "What do you want, Yasir?"

He shrugs, standing two feet away from the table I

claimed all for myself. I notice his hair is done in this mussed hairstyle like, well, Izyaan's. At first glance, you really can mistake him for his cousin. Coincidence?

"I came to pick up an order for my dad and saw you sitting here. Alone. I don't think I've ever seen you without Safiya before."

"Are you following me?" I ask. "Because it sure feels like it. You're here almost every day."

Yasir holds up his hands in surrender. "No! My dad's office is here in the town center. It's the big glass building near the parking garage. Top floor. I come to work with him sometimes. He doesn't let me do anything, though, so I get bored and invite my friends to come hang out."

Well, that explains a lot. "I didn't know your dad worked here."

"His office is really nice," Yasir says, suddenly putting on a showy grin. "There's free soda and snacks. You can hang out there anytime. If you want," he adds as an afterthought. If Yasir's trying to impress me, he's not doing a very good job. He was this close to being okay in my books just now, but he had to go and open his mouth again.

"I'm out," I say, sliding out of the booth.

"Wait." He blocks my path and I quickly raise my

half-eaten plate of crepes as a buffer between us. "Why were you crying?"

"I wasn't," I say tersely.

"You were."

"Even if I was, it's none of your business! Now move." I make a shooing gesture with one hand.

"Okay, okay. I was trying to help. Sorry, I'm bad at this. This whole making friends thing. A lot of kids don't want to come near me because they're scared of my mom. She's really controlling and always ruling over my life. And my dad's always working, so I only come with him to get out of the house and away from her." I want to say that maybe *he's* the problem but stop at his bummed expression. I don't want to hear about Yasir's family problems, but I should show the guy some sympathy, I guess. I can't imagine having Gabina Auntie for a mom. It sounds like a nightmare.

"That sucks," I say. "But why do you need new friends? You already have three. Four, since there's Izyaan, too."

Yasir rolls his eyes. "He's my cousin. That doesn't count. And I'm pretty sure Abdul, Mustafa, and Shezi only hang out with me because they get cool perks."

I have no clue how to respond to that, so I stare down at my crepes awkwardly. I don't have time for Yasir and his personal issues. I already have too much on my plate as it is. After my complete fumble today, I have to work twice as hard to prove myself to Amma. I promised Abu I would be a good helper, not the opposite.

"Look, Yasir," I finally manage. "We can't be friends. We're too . . . different," I say, floundering.

"So are you and Safiya," he points out. The way he says it makes me want to ask him what exactly he means by that, but I zip it. It feels like it won't matter what I say. He's always got a comeback.

"We actually have a lot in common," says Yasir. "Both of our families are super religious." He acts like *religious* is a bad word, and it ticks me off. I want to get in his face and scream that my parents are nothing like his. I don't know what he's going off of—outward appearances or something else. Either way, his comment doesn't sit right with me. My parents always taught me it's the inside of a person that counts most. And Yasir and his mom are both rotten to the core.

"Yeah. They are. And unlike you, I have nothing against it," I say, hoping that will finally knock some sense into him. I shoulder past him so that I don't have to hear his response and walk away.

I have more important things to do than stand around

fending Yasir off. If I'm going to be serious about getting back on track at the store and designing the bridesmaid dresses, then I need to focus. I can't let Yasir throw me off. For the first time, I'm really considering telling a grown-up about his behavior. But who? I can't tell Amma and Abu. I don't want to add to their worries. The only other adult I can think of is Sister Ambreen, but it wouldn't be fair to make her own nephew look bad when Amarah and Izyaan's family has done so much for us. Sister Ambreen would for sure tell Amma. And what if I *am* drawing Yasir's attention due to the way I dress? Otherwise, why would he keep talking to me after all the hints I dropped? None of the adults will take me seriously if it's my fault, and the only way not to take the blame is for me to dress differently. Un-Ainy-like.

Let's not forget that Yasir knows about my crush on Izyaan because I was careless enough to admit that to him. He could rat me out as payback whenever. I don't need Amma thinking I'm doing anything wrong. Not with everything else going on in our lives. I'm *not* doing anything wrong. Right? I just can't help how I feel. And who knows if anyone will even believe me with Yasir's family's social status. I bet his friends would back him up, too. It's my word against all of theirs.

If he's here at the town center all the time, then there's only one other solution. I can't leave the store. Like, ever. No more lunch breaks outside. Which means I'm going to have to keep flaking on Safiya to avoid running into him.

Safiya will understand. We're not best friends for nothing.

CHAPTER 14

Safiya does not understand. I'm pretty sure she's ready to strangle me for blowing her off again and again. It's been a whole week since I last saw her. I can't remember the last time that happened. Safiya won't even come into the store to hang out anymore. And now I'm breaking it to her that I'm missing Algeria's Independence Day with her family the day of.

> **Safiya:** YOU'RE NOT COMING?! Why?? My jid-dati has Algerian clothes and everything ready for you to wear!!

> **Me:** I'm sorry, the store's just so busy and I still haven't finished the bridesmaid dresses ☹

Which is the truth. I've been working hard to prove myself to Amma after my major screwup last week and I can't afford to slack off. My free time is minimal, so I haven't had time to work on the designs. Even though my reason is honest now, it sounds pathetic after days of feeding Safiya weak excuses about why I won't have lunch with her in the town center anymore.

> **Safiya:** Idk Ainy it's like you pulled out this brand-new personality. You're not you anymore. It's not fair that you keep choosing your new job over me! We made our plans first!

Our text thread goes dead after that. That last one was a real gut punch. I consider telling her how dire the situation with my dadi is and how Bajjo working two jobs to help support us is hard . . . but I don't know. All I've been doing nowadays is hiding. Hiding at the store, where I'm needed, and at home. I'm too much of a baby to go out in public. If I do, I take turns wearing the same three boring outfits in hopes that at least Yasir will be put off. But that's not stopping him from occasionally messaging me on Scope. I leave him on read every single time, and he still won't get a clue.

Clearly, I'm cursed because I'm invisible to everyone else. Amma, Bajjo, and Kashif have a set routine and I'm just an extra on the movie set of their lives. I don't even get a chance to talk to Abu that much.

Basically, nothing is going according to plan.

———◆◆———

I'm at Naseerah's Almari on the Sunday after Algeria's Independence Day, sitting at the counter in front of a blank page. Yup. I skipped going to the Messaoudis' house and have nothing to show for it. Regret sits heavy in my stomach. My pencil sits untouched on the counter. I don't know why I'm acting like it's going to bite my fingers off if I pick it up. I'm paying more attention to the calendar ticking down the days like some kind of doom clock. I've already wasted two weeks. It's a quiet, slow day at the store. I should be taking advantage of it. Instead, my mind keeps wheeling around, trying and failing to switch my brain's light bulb back on, but no dice. Something keeps fusing the bulb. At this point, I wish the bridesmaid dresses would draw themselves because I'm clearly not cut out for this. And then I get mad at myself for stressing out this much trying to design something special for Gabina Auntie. It's not like she deserves it. Both she and her son are awful people.

"Ainy?" Amma comes to stand in the doorway dividing the back room from the front of the store. I cover the empty page with my arms guiltily. "Just checking in. Everything all right up here?" she asks.

She's keeping an eye on me. I knew Amma wasn't going to trust me after last week's mix-up. That's why I have to get the design for these dresses right. My dignity depends on it.

I give Amma a thumbs-up.

"Good. Do you have any new designs cooking up for the bridesmaid dresses?" Amma asks the question casually, but I can detect the hint of concern looping through her words. Her gaze travels to the calendar open on the front desk's computer. I know what she's thinking. Five weeks left until our deadline, and only two weeks left until she's going to take the job off my hands if I don't come through.

"I'm . . . onto something," I lie. Shame bolts through me, but the fear of failure has me in a stronger chokehold. "I'll show you when it's ready."

There's a short but pronounced pause before Amma says, "Okay. Can I ask for a favor?" She nestles her right wrist in her left hand. "Can you please run down to the sporting goods store and buy me a wrist brace? All this cutting and sewing is making my hand ache. I'll watch the front desk."

I'm on my feet in an instant. After Amma hands me her card, I give her a tight, apologetic squeeze. Then I'm out the door. It's only when I get there that I remember I've never been inside an athletic store. The place has two huge floors. It's going to be like finding a needle in a haystack.

I scratch my head, turning in circles and reading all the signs like they're written in a different language. The farther I walk through the various sections, the more lost I become. I didn't know this many sports existed in real life! Do wrist braces count as accessories? What the heck is athleisure? People dress their literal spitting babies in expensive brands like Nike and Adidas? I picture Noor slobbering applesauce all over a forty-dollar onesie and I die a little inside.

"I think you're in the wrong store," comes a teasing voice. "All the cool fashion-y brands are on the other side of the shopping center."

I stop in my tracks, whipping to the right to find Izyaan beaming at me from between two aisles of athletic footwear.

"Hey, what are you doing here?" As soon as the words leap off my tongue, I realize (1) he's shopping for shoes, duh, and (2) it's more realistic for him to be here than me.

"Killing time," Izyaan says with a shrug. "My dad's getting a haircut, so I'm just looking around." He scrunches his mouth at the rows of footwear. "Too bad this place doesn't sell fencing equipment. They don't even have the shoes for it. Mine are falling apart."

"Oh, that sucks." Meanwhile, my heart is stomping around on my insides. I try to act natural. Like I come here all the time. From what I know, fencing is a pretty niche sport. I didn't know it was *that* niche, though. Playing a hyperspecialized sport makes Izyaan even more attractive in my eyes. It makes him stand out.

I dig my fingernails into the palm of my hands. *Pull yourself together, Ainy!*

A funny look enters Izyaan's eyes at whatever cartoonish expression I'm wearing, and for a terrible second I'm sure he knows my secret. That Yasir told him and he's just been keeping quiet. But then, he wouldn't be talking to me right now if he knew. Right? There's no way Izyaan actually likes me back. Maybe if my life were a fairy tale, which it isn't. I'm no princess.

"So," Izyaan muses, stuffing his fists into his jean pockets and rocking on his heels. "Why are you here? Aren't you supposed to be at work?"

"I am," I say, combing through a tiny knot in my hair with my fingers. "Amma sent me here to buy her a wrist brace. Problem is, I don't know where they keep them."

His face falls. "Oh man. Poor Naseerah Auntie. I know where they are. Follow me."

I practically float behind him as he leads me down the escalators to a wall of braces. Ankle braces, knee braces, shoulder-support braces, sleeves.

"Jeez," I mutter.

"You'd be surprised how many ways you can get hurt," Izyaan says casually. "I want to be a sports physical therapist one day. To help people recover from their injuries."

My heart melts into a pile of goop. "That's awesome. You're gonna be so good at it," I say, and I really mean it. Izyaan has the kind of aura that makes you want to trust him. People are drawn to him like magnets. At school, he's always surrounded by friends. He doesn't even have a defined clique. I see him hanging around with all different types of kids. The popular crowd, the quiet, nerdy ones, the athletes. You name it. Bajjo's always saying how colleges want "well-rounded individuals" and I wonder if that's what they mean.

I locate a black wrist brace and hold it up triumphantly. "Got it. Thanks for your help."

"Anytime," Izyaan says. "Hey, you're going next weekend, right?"

"Next weekend?" I echo, not following. And then it hits me and I want to slam my head against the nearest shelf. "Family Day," I groan.

Izyaan looks confused by my misery. "I thought you loved Family Day."

Yeah, he's right. I do. That's the issue. It's my and Safiya's favorite tradition. Once a year over the summer, the interfaith community gets together at the theme park for a whole day. As a result of the big groups, tickets are dirt cheap. Safiya and I are hard-core about Family Day. We've been going together for years. The Khalids are always there. Unfortunately, Yasir's family is, too. In the past, that didn't matter. But this year it's different. Safiya hasn't mentioned Family Day recently, and I wonder if it's because she's lost all hope of me going. The idea of skipping out on Family Day is tragic, but I think I have to. I can't go with Yasir still on the loose and the bridesmaid dresses sitting unfinished. How am I going to break that to Safiya, though? She is extra excited about it this year because her parents are going to leave Noor with her grandparents so that they can finally spend some time together like they used to before. That is, without a wailing baby in tow.

Wait. *Parents!* They're going to be crawling all over the place! Yasir wouldn't dare pull a trick with so many adults around. And the park is huge. What are the chances that I'll run into him and his friends anyway? We run in completely different circles. Besides, Yasir probably finds the whole event loserish. A theme park full of people from the religious community? I'm sure he'd rather stay home and the only reason he comes is because Gabina Auntie makes him.

I smile to myself. You know what? Maybe I need a break. Time to relax so that my old creative spark will return. I've been so burned out by all the stuff crowding my brain. Maybe I can conquer this annoying designer's block if I just let it all go. Stop hiding and have fun again. It's just *one* day. Plus, I miss Safiya a lot. I've been a crappy friend and I have to make it up to her. No matter what happens, I can't desert her again. I need to get my creative juices back without losing my best friend. Family Day could be the key to setting everything right.

"You're going, aren't you?" Izyaan asks again. I could be imagining it, but he looks kind of nervous about my answer.

"Oh, I'll be there," I say, waving a silly-you-even-asked hand at Izyaan. "I wouldn't miss Family Day for anything."

CHAPTER 15

The next Saturday, Izyaan's dad makes the two-hour drive to the amusement park with Sister Ambreen riding shotgun; me, Bajjo, and Amarah squished together in the middle row; and Kashif and Izyaan in the very back of the van. Amma didn't come, because Saturdays are her busiest days, but she assured us she could handle the store on her own for one day.

I decided to surprise Safiya, so she has no idea that I'm coming. I figured me showing up would be the best kind of apology for the way I've been treating her. When the roller coaster crest comes into view ahead, I let out all the air in my lungs. We pull into the packed parking lot right as Zuhr starts and find a spot way in the back. We take turns praying on thin travel salat rugs with the sun baking our backs. When we're done, our little group makes its way to the park's entrance. Safiya and her parents are waiting on a bench right outside. Her eyes go round when she sees me approaching.

I hook my arm through hers. "Surprise!"

Safiya gives me a flat look. "Wow. It's a miracle." And she pulls herself out of my grasp, crossing her arms while facing the adults double-checking that everyone's here.

Okay, I deserved that.

Safiya's mom pinches my cheek hello, and I wonder if it's just a habit. I'd probably start randomly pinching people's cheeks too if I had a squishy baby to play with all day.

"You guys left Noor at your grandma's?" I casually ask Safiya in the ticket/bag check line.

She shoots me an annoyed look. "My nani's. Mama was already getting emotional when we dropped her off," she complains, straightening the yellow cap she's got on over her hijab.

I want to tell her that's normal, but I swallow it before it slips out. Safiya might push me off a ride if I say that to her right now. Instead, I roll my eyes in sympathy. "Oh, come on. It's only for a few hours!"

"Right? They gave me a whole lecture on the way here about how I need to be more helpful. I'm her big sister and she's going to look up to me blah blah blah. She's literally a baby. What does she care anyway? Ugh, I couldn't even listen to my audiobook in peace."

"I'm sorry," I say, and it's for her miserable car ride as much as my neglecting her all this time.

"Why are you here?" Safiya asks. I don't miss the resentment in her tone. "Don't you have more important things to do?"

"This is important, too," I say feebly.

The apology in my voice melts some of the hardness in her expression. "If you'd told me you were coming, you could've ridden with us," Safiya says before she passes through the metal detectors.

When I join her on the other side, I say, "I wasn't sure if you wanted to be stuck in a car with me."

"Yeah. You probably would've ignored me there, too." Only the small smile tugging at her lips betrays the fact that she's more teasing than serious.

Guilt knots my stomach. "Safiya, I'm really—"

"Forget it, Ainy." Safiya acts like she's going to say more, but she doesn't when she notices me fanning my face and looking around. She unhelpfully points behind us. "Izyaan's over there."

"Cut it out!" I karate chop her hand down before he

sees. In reality, I'm on the lookout for Yasir. I recognize familiar faces from our masjid as well as our local church and synagogue. Everyone's finding their friends and family and talking about what they've been up to since the summer started. No Yasir in sight. Good. I just have to stay one step ahead of him the whole day and all will be well.

Once everyone's through the security line, the four parents, me, Safiya, Amarah, Bajjo, Izyaan, and Kashif gather in front of the big fountain marking the park's entrance for a group picture.

"Salaam, everyone," comes a voice that makes my photo-ready smile melt right off my face. Gabina Auntie is making her way toward us. Yasir, Mustafa, Shezi, and Abdul are trailing behind her, already braying like a bunch of donkeys over some video they're watching on Abdul's phone.

Sister Ambreen gives her sister-in-law a tight smile. "Walaikumusalam. Sorry to hear that Jamil couldn't make it."

"He had an appointment with a very important client. Couldn't reschedule," Gabina Auntie says with no remorse. Her stern gaze instantly falls on me and Bajjo before I can think to hide. "Girls. How are you? How are the bridesmaid dresses coming along? Your mother will still be able to meet the deadline, I hope?"

"Oh yeah! For sure! They're going great! Nearly done!" My face feels like it's going to crack in half. Bajjo snaps her head at me uncertainly.

"Can you send me a preview? My niece is getting nervous and would feel better with a tiny glimpse of how they're going to turn out."

Sure, if her niece wants a glimpse at big ole nothing. I twist my hands together painfully. It occurs to me that Gabina Auntie has no idea that I'm supposed to be designing the dresses. How would she react if she knew Amma had designated the task to a twelve-year-old?

Safiya narrows her eyes at me skeptically. Right, *she* thinks I've been spending all the time that I'm not with her designing said dresses when I've really been stumbling through the dark and crisis-eating lots of Sour Patch Kids instead.

"All of our designs are back at the store," Bajjo interjects. "We don't have access to them at the moment." For real, I could kiss her right now.

"Why don't we focus on why we're here?" Sister Ambreen offers. "Rides! Wristband check, everyone!" We all lift our hands above our heads. "Great. Who's ready to have some fun?" She pumps a fist in the air and makes a whooping noise while we bob our heads yes.

"Mom, they're too old for that now," says Amarah. "Kulsoom and I are going on the Booster Seat before the line gets too long." The Booster Seat is exactly what it sounds like: a roller coaster with seats built to look like booster seats. Ironically, it's also the tallest and fastest ride in the whole park. Definitely not for babies.

"Keep your locations on!" Sister Ambreen calls after Bajjo and Amarah as they break off from us. They'll probably find their other teen friends and we won't see them for the rest of the day.

"We've got these two." Safiya's mom puts her arms around me and Safiya. "Kashif, do you want to join us?"

"Of course not," Gabina Auntie butts in. "He should stay with the other boys."

Warning bells go off in my head and, against my better judgment, I look over at Yasir. Oh no. Why is he staring at me so intensely? *Stop that!* If I pretend not to notice him, maybe he'll just fade into the background. I tell myself to relax. Izyaan will be with Kashif. He treats him like his own little brother. As much as I want to protectively cling to Kashif, he's not going to turn into an insolent brat by hanging around with the other boys for a few hours. Besides, there are three adults chaperoning them. Kashif's basically got a whole security force.

Still, I can feel myself shaking as Safiya's parents lead us down one path and the boys go the other. I can't help looking back. Yasir's got his head turned like he is watching me go. In that moment, I get a very bad feeling that he isn't planning on going anywhere. I'm stuck with him, this lurking shadow that keeps on following me around. And I have no idea what I did to deserve it.

CHAPTER 16

Safiya and I collapse on a bench right outside the Drop Tower on wobbly legs.

"That was awesome," I pant.

Safiya's dad unsteadily sits down next to her, pressing a palm against his forehead. "I can't handle these rides like I used to." He groans. "Wow, this headache."

"I think it's time for a break," Suha Auntie says lightly. After two hours in this brutal heat, her makeup is still flawless.

Both my and Safiya's faces are flushed crimson. As usual, we worked—or rather, rode—ourselves to the point of breaking. Islam Uncle upgraded us to fast lane passes so we didn't have to spend as much time waiting in all the long lines. That meant we got to go on the popular rides multiple times, until we both got bored of them or felt like puking or passing out. We've been having so much fun that we didn't even pause to catch our breaths until now. Best of all, Safiya's back to her old self.

And I've thought about Yasir exactly zero times. Overall, this trip's been worth it so far.

"Can we eat lunch now?" Safiya complains, clutching her stomach. "I'm starving."

"I actually just got a message from the others in the group chat. They're headed for the pizzeria. It's a five-minute walk from here. Think you can make it?" asks Suha Auntie.

Safiya and I try standing and wind up dramatically falling back down while loudly whining about sore feet, sweaty armpits, and in Safiya's case, a damp underscarf.

"Maybe we should rent strollers for them," Islam Uncle suggests with amusement. "Since they're acting like big *babies*."

"You were the one complaining about having a headache after a few rides like an old man," Safiya gibes.

"A few? I think we've hit almost all of them at this point," says Islam Uncle. "What's left? The Teacups? Oh, sorry. That's only for grown kids, not little—youch!" Safiya smacks her dad's arm and he spins away snickering.

Their exchange makes me miss Abu. I try not to linger on the feeling, though. If I let that one thing slip out from the corner of my mind where I stuffed everything to enjoy this day, then the rest will come avalanching out.

We're able to walk to the pizzeria after rehydrating and a few more minutes of rest. The AC's blasting but the diner still feels warm and stuffy because of how many people are inside. Through one of the windows, we spot Sister Ambreen's group spread out at two tables under the shaded patio.

"You guys go on. I have to take this," says Suha Auntie. She holds up her phone to show that Safiya's nani is calling. She's been peppering Suha Auntie with questions about Noor through call and text since we got to the park. Safiya shoots her mom laser eyes, but Islam Uncle leads us away before she can take Suha Auntie's phone and hurl it in the nearest trash can.

"You made it," Sister Ambreen says when we join them outside. "Dig in. We ordered plenty of food."

I appreciate the distraction and the fact that Kashif's seated with us so that I don't have to pay attention to the boys at the table next to us. Everyone definitely looks like they spent some time in the sun with their hair all slicked back with sweat. Izyaan looks up from his pizza briefly to meet my eyes at the exact same time that Yasir notices me. I glance away quickly. I chew on a slice of gooey cheese pizza while Safiya and I go through pictures and videos on our phones to decide which ones to upload to Scope.

"I need more napkins," says Kashif. A chunky glob of tomato sauce slides off his chin and spatters the front of his shirt. Kashif's eyes go wide. "Ugh!"

"It's okay," Sister Ambreen says. "Go to the bathroom and wash it off."

"I'll take him," Yasir offers. I drop my pizza and turn my head toward him incredulously. Was he eavesdropping on us? Even Safiya, Izyaan, Abdul, Shezi, and Mustafa are giving Yasir weird looks, like he offered to wipe Kashif's butt.

"He's nine," I say too fiercely. "He doesn't need you to take him."

"Someone should go with him," Yasir pushes. "There are too many people. He could get lost."

Gabina Auntie looks at her son like he's a complete angel. "That's so kind of you, beta. Yes, Kashif. Go with Yasir bhai. He will help you clean off."

I can't do anything but watch helplessly as Yasir takes Kashif by the hand. Izyaan seems kind of sad that his big brother role was hijacked. As soon as they head for the bathroom inside the pizzeria, Abdul's, Mustafa's, and Shezi's gazes land on me. All three of them are wearing the same knowing expression. Honestly, Yasir couldn't have been more obvious if he tried. It was just *tomato sauce*.

It feels like a radioactive spider bites me and instills me with courage I didn't know I had. I wipe my greasy fingers with a napkin and shoot to my feet. "I have to use the bathroom, too."

Safiya looks up from her phone, alarmed. "Uh, okay. Do you want me to go with y—?"

I'm already gone before she can finish her sentence. Inside, I weave through the dense crowd, trying to remember where I saw signs for the bathroom when we first entered. There are dozens of different lines in here for food, so it takes me a minute to figure out which ones are for the bathroom and find them.

I march right up to Yasir outside the men's room and yank Kashif away from him. "Stay away from him!" I exclaim. "Just stop already."

"Stop what?" Yasir asks, sounding truly puzzled.

"Whatever this is! You trying to weasel your way into my life! Leave Kashif out of this!" I'm yelling now. People are beginning to stare at us.

"What are you talking about? I was just trying to give

Izyaan a break! He's been looking after him all day," Yasir says innocently.

I fold my arms over my chest. "Are you sure this is about Izyaan?"

Yasir blushes. *Ding. Ding. Ding.* "I don't get why you're so mad. I was trying to be nice."

"Why on earth do you think I need you to be nice to me?" I ask, beyond frustrated at this point. "I don't need you. Why don't you get it? We. Are. Not. Friends."

"Whoa! That was *harsh*!" Abdul's voice sends my blood skittering through my veins. I didn't even notice him, Mustafa, and Shezi sneak up on us. "Ainy Zain knows how to be mean?"

"What's going on?" Now Safiya and Izyaan appear and Safiya elbows her way up to me. "Why's everyone just standing around?"

"Why do you have to barge into everything?" Abdul jabs at her.

"Excuse me?" Safiya whirls on him. A tiny tornado ready to trample him. "She's *my* friend. The real question is, why are *you* here?"

"We need to wash our hands," says Mustafa. "But Yasir and Ainy are holding up the line." His smile is razor sharp. "Come on, you two. Go hold hands over there or something. We won't bother you."

I stop breathing. I don't know who's more shocked: me, Yasir, Safiya, or Izyaan.

"How dare you!" Without warning, Safiya's hands come up and shove Mustafa, who stumbles back a couple of steps. Mustafa's face is so red you could dip a paintbrush in it. He marches forward, and for a second I actually think he's going to push Safiya right back, but Izyaan blocks him.

"You guys need to stop this," Izyaan says. Safiya and Mustafa are on either side of him, glaring at each other like they're ready to duke it out. Neither one wants to back down. Izyaan looks like he's desperately trying to figure out a way to defuse the situation, but his mind can't work fast enough.

"She pushed me first!" Mustafa struggles against Izyaan's outstretched arms.

Kashif trembles next to me. He looks like he's fighting back tears.

"Knock it off! You're scaring Kashif!" I yell at them.

"Man up, kid," Shezi says in Kashif's direction.

What happens next is a blur. All I know is that Shezi's

words make a fuse blow inside me. I'm this close to lunging at him when it happens. Yasir's hand arcs up and grabs the top of my arm. My whole vision shrinks down to that one touch. I wait, but he doesn't move his hand. Spine prickling, I throw him off. Horror and a sense of wrongness twists in my stomach. I've *never* let a boy touch me before, and I'm not about to start now. The least Yasir can do is apologize. There's no way he didn't notice that.

"Don't touch me!" I shriek, literally shaking.

"What are you all doing?"

The sharp voice makes all of us turn at the exact same time. Gabina Auntie is there with her hands on her hips, looking for all the world like a strict school principal ready to dish out detention. Her presence sets all of us on edge. I try to imagine what the scene looks like from her point of view. Izyaan braced between Safiya and Mustafa. Kashif near tears. Yasir hovering so close behind me that a slight movement could make our arms brush again. Without a doubt, this looks really, really bad. No one says a word. Gabina Auntie's expression makes me squirm and I'm one hundred percent sure she's getting the wrong idea.

"You two." Gabina Auntie points at me and Safiya. "Go to the other line."

"But they—" I start.

"*Now.*"

Why is she singling *us* out? Safiya tugs my elbow urgently and I reluctantly let Kashif go. Safiya and I wait in line for the girls' bathroom. I didn't have to use it before, but now I do. Not to use the toilet, though. As soon as Safiya and I step inside, I burst into tears at the way this whole day has gone down in flames. I'm so angry and embarrassed that it feels like it's going to burn through my skin.

Safiya hugs me in front of the sink, rubbing my back soothingly. She calls the boys a whole bunch of rude names that I'm sure any adult would balk at. "They're a bunch of horrible jerks. I can't believe them. You? Like *Yasir*? Not even in their dreams."

Oh, she's got it the other way around. Safiya doesn't know what's been happening ever since school let out. All the ways that Yasir keeps popping up and ruining my summer, my life. I desperately want to share everything with my best friend. Get it all off my chest. But it's like every time I try, my courage deserts me. Because what if I am doing something to call attention to myself and I'm just not aware of it? Safiya's already a confident hijabi with zero insecurities. None of the boys bother her. I'm ashamed and can't help but feel like I'm bringing this on to myself. Safiya would never send the wrong signals. She would've figured out how to solve this problem right away if she'd been in my shoes. She wouldn't be a scaredy-cat like me who can't stick up for herself.

I stare at my tearstained face in the mirror over Safiya's shoulder. I wish Yasir hadn't started thinking I was pretty. I wish things would go back to the way they were *before.* When I didn't exist to him. A nobody. I would do anything to be a nobody if it meant Yasir stopped liking me.

He doesn't want a hijabi.

Aaira Auntie's voice from weeks ago smacks my eardrums. Her implication that some boys nowadays don't want to go for girls who wear hijab. An idea begins to take shape in my mind. What if now's the time? What if this is my sign? Given Yasir's general disdain for religion, the hijab could be the answer to all my problems. I mean, this scenario isn't how I imagined myself starting to wear it, but maybe all it takes is putting it on to gain confidence in the first place.

What's Izyaan gonna say, though? What if he *stops liking you, too?*

I bite my lip. His mom wears it. His sister wears it. What problem could he possibly have? I just want to fill the fashion-size hole in my life and beat this designer's block. But first, I need Yasir out of my hair (uh, pun intended?). And I have just the person in my life who can teach me how.

"Safiya." I sniffle, pulling back to look her square in the face. "I need your help."

CHAPTER 17

I haven't been to Safiya's house in ages. So when Bajjo drops me off at the Messaoudis' for dinner after closing up at Naseerah's Almari the Monday after Family Day, I'm thrown off by the playpen, the hoard of baby toys, the high chair, the bouncer, the baby swing. Their house looks like a daycare threw up in it.

Suha Auntie's struggling to feed Noor a spoonful of applesauce in the kitchen when Safiya lets me in, mumbling apologies under her breath about the state of the house.

"Asalamualaikum, Ainy! It's so nice to see you! We miss having you around," Suha Auntie chimes, like she didn't spend the entire day with me two days ago. "We made korma for dinner! I know how much you love it."

I wiggle my fingers and make silly faces at Noor across the room. She squeals with delight. Safiya, on the other hand, is not keen to stick around for much longer.

"Mama, can we use your salon?" asks Safiya. "I'm teaching Ainy how to—do the perfect winged eyeliner. We want to use the big makeup mirror downstairs. Is that okay?" I give Safiya a secretive smile at the save. I told her I don't want anyone to know about me trying the hijab because my intentions aren't set in stone yet. I'm just testing the waters for now. That's why we met up here instead of at my place. For the privacy.

"Sure. Try not to break anything. I'll call you girls up when it's time to eat. *Noor!*" Suha Auntie laments when Noor knocks the bowl out of her hand and it lands upside down in Noor's lap. Noor immediately fists clumps of applesauce into her mouth, smearing it all over her face, hair, and bib while Suha Auntie shakes her head and sighs.

Safiya practically flings both of us down the stairs to her basement, her thick hair bouncing ahead of me like springs. Safiya's hair is dark-brown-basically-black like Suha Auntie's, but her tight curls are from her dad's side of the family.

Downstairs in Suha Auntie's home beauty salon, Safiya flips on the lights.

A massage and facial bed takes up the center of the room. In the corner, a washbasin stands behind a leather recliner. Another styling chair is opposite it in front of a floor-to-ceiling mirror mounted with dozens of little lights. There's a whole shelf of expensive hair and skin care products. Suha Auntie's makeup vanity is clean and organized. The air smells like a mix of perfume, essential oils, and powder.

"Sit down, Ainy Zain." Safiya pats the chair facing the mirror. I climb onto it, sitting dutifully with my hands in my lap while Safiya stands in front of me with her ankles crossed. "So. You want to be a hijabi, but you don't know where to start?" Safiya asks, imitating an infomercial voice-over. I giggle.

Safiya hasn't asked me even once why I've decided to give the hijab a shot now. She just jumped on board like the supportive friend that she is, even though I haven't been returning the favor lately.

"Step one," Safiya continues, reaching behind her for something. That's when I notice the stuff lined up on the vanity that doesn't usually belong. "Choosing an under-scarf." She holds up two different-colored hijab caps. "You don't have to wear one, but they're great because they hold your scarf in place so it's not sliding off your head. The best material is silk or satin, but really, anything goes as long as you remember to take care of your hair. Also, pins are out. Magnets are all the rage. No more holes!"

I've watched Bajjo try to perfect different hijab styles for years, but I didn't realize being a hijabi involved so much maintenance. I thought the hardest part was finding one to match your outfit. It feels like I should be taking notes, so I listen to Safiya with my undivided attention.

"Don't worry. I put all of this in the presentation I made for you, so you don't have to memorize it." *Presentation?* Wow, Safiya has gone above and beyond on this project. But that's Safiya for you. Always prepared.

"Since you're a beginner, you could go with a pre-sewn hijab. But then you'd look like a little kid playing dress-up. Never mind. We're going all in," says Safiya. "First things first. Tie your hair. Try to make a low ponytail as much as possible. It puts less tension on your scalp." Safiya grabs a hairbrush and works it through my hair. It's long enough that she can get a short ponytail out of it. Next, she shows me how to slip on the underscarf. Once that's sitting on my head, Safiya picks up a gray scarf that I recognize as one of hers. "Your scarf's texture matters a lot. Some are made of a light material, and some are heavier and don't slip off as easy. You'll look more put-together if you iron it first. It all depends on what you want. Chiffon's pretty, but it's hard to fiddle around with, so we're going with good old woven."

When I go to the masjid, I always wear a hijab as a sign of respect, but I just throw a scarf around my head, wrap it a few times, and tuck the end away under my chin. Now that feels kind of sloppy, like I was a kid riding a bike with training wheels. But Safiya's advanced.

"I'm going to show you a super easy style," Safiya says, continuing the tutorial. "Fold it from the front a little bit, like this." She folds the scarf lengthwise a couple of inches and brings it around my head, setting it down so that both sides are dangling in equal length down my chest. She takes both pieces and uses tiny magnets to secure the scarf underneath my chin. "Your face is more heart-shaped versus my round, so I'm going to make yours a teeny bit tighter. Okay, now we're going to take one end of your scarf and throw it over your shoulder. Grab the inside part and bring it over, otherwise you'll get this weird twisty thing. This way, it hides your neck, too. Leave this last half down so it covers your chest. You can spread it out a little if you want." Safiya concentrates as she plays around with my hijab until she achieves the look she wants. Then she steps back and looks me over. "And voilà! Introducing Ainy Zain, hijabi edition!"

I stare at myself in the mirror. The first thought that races through my mind with a dull ache is *I look like Bajjo.* What she used to look like, at least. I feel like a balloon with a hole in it. Then I realize Safiya's waiting for my reaction and I refocus on my reflection. I look different. Still me, but another version of me. Less . . . noticeable? I guess that's the whole point. For some reason I feel bad. There's this strange tug of guilt in my heart when I peer at myself, but I can't explain why.

"I like it," I say, checking myself out from different angles.

"Honey, you look so cute!" Safiya squeals. The moral encouragement is enough to break me out of my funk and smile big at her.

"You think so?" I ask her.

"Totally. So what're you thinking? When do you want to try wearing it outside?"

Already? I don't have a good reason to say no. Tomorrow's as good a day as any to give it a whirl. Yasir is sure to be at the town center with his friends as always. I need to know as soon as possible if my plan will work. The sooner I get Yasir off my back, the faster the rest of my life will get back on track.

"Tomorrow," I say before I lose my nerve. "But don't

tell Amma and Bajjo." If things don't go according to plan, I don't want either of them to question what's going on.

Safiya nods, and it feels dirty that I'm hiding the fact that my intentions aren't sincere when she's going to such lengths to help me. I turn to look at myself in the mirror again, and I still can't get over the fact that it feels like I'm *missing* something.

"Safiya." A question sits ready at the tip of my tongue, but then Suha Auntie calls us from upstairs saying that dinner's ready.

"Just wanted to say thanks for doing this," I say, mentally trashing the question. I'd always imagined Bajjo being the one to teach me how to put the hijab on properly, but I'm glad it ended up being Safiya.

I carefully unravel the scarf, take the magnets out, and remove the underscarf to give back to Safiya. "We'll practice some more after we eat," she says, throwing her arms around me as we leave the salon. "You'll be a pro before you know it."

We hear Noor's screams get louder as we climb the stairs. *I feel you, Noor,* I think. For all my confidence that my plan will work, I want to kick my legs and scream at the heavens, too.

CHAPTER 18

Safiya and I whisk away during my lunch break the next day. We head to a diner bathroom first. Safiya digs through her bag and takes out a small velvet pouch with magnet pins, a neutral-color underscarf, and a beautiful rose-gold hijab Safiya let me choose from her closet last night. It's not *my* First Day of Hijab hijab because, well, is that really today? What if it's not? I didn't want to waste it.

I follow Safiya's instructions from memory and secure the hijab around my head in front of the bathroom mirror. I chose a cute outfit for the occasion: a flowy white blouse with statement fringe sleeves and elastic-waist black-and-white plaid pants that are *this* close to getting too short on me, but they pass the test today. I've also got on my nicest sandals.

"You look amazing!" Safiya says, and I soak up her praise like a sponge to fight off the nausea threatening to empty my stomach.

"Ready?" Safiya asks, bowing toward the door.

I take a deep breath. Here goes nothing.

My feet feel ten times heavier than usual as I lead the way out of the bathroom.

"Don't sweat it. You're doing great," Safiya says when I've only made it about ten steps. She pushes me the rest of the way out so I'm in full view of the restaurant, and I freeze. I squeeze my eyes shut and brace for the weight of hundreds of eyes to fall on me. For the sky to open up through the glass ceiling and shine a spotlight down on me. Set me on fire.

But nothing happens. No dramatic, earth-shattering event, except for a little boy crying to my right because he dropped his fries all over the floor.

"Let's find a table," Safiya pipes up, and treads ahead of me. I follow hesitantly, wringing my hands. My eyes keep skipping around the room in fear that someone's going to pick me out of the crowd and just . . . stare. Make a face. Judge.

Safiya and I sit down and order food. "So, how do you

feel?" Safiya asks around a mouthful of gyro while mine sits untouched on the table in front of me.

I shrug. "I don't know. I thought I'd feel different."

"Different how?"

I wrestle with how to put it. "I guess I thought I'd feel more of a spiritual spark? Some kind of instant connection to Allah?"

Safiya blinks at me, parsing my words. "It's hijab, Ainy. Not a magic wand."

I chance another glance around the room. Everyone's in their own world, eating, talking, texting, taking pictures. We're just two girls having lunch in the town center. Some of my uneasiness falls away and I sit up straighter. Safiya grins, but then her eyes roam to the side and she lets out a groan. "Oh, look. Our favorite people."

I don't have to look to know who she's talking about, but I do anyway. The whole gang's here, just as I suspected. Yasir, Abdul, Shezi, Mustafa, and . . . *ugh, why couldn't you stay home today, Izyaan?* My earlier dread returns and I slink deeper into the booth.

"Ignore them," Safiya says, using a fork to stab at the filling falling out of her gyro. She's still prickly about what happened on Family Day. Unfortunately, I kind of need the boys to notice me. Especially Yasir. But I don't want to make the first move.

Lucky for me, it doesn't take long for us to get spotted. But it's not by Yasir. One minute, Izyaan's on his phone hovering by a table the boys have chosen a couple of rows away and the next, his eyes flick up from his screen and land in our direction. He obviously recognizes Safiya, but he frowns at me. Confusion plays across his expression like he's trying to solve a difficult equation in his head. *He doesn't know it's me.* But I pinpoint the exact moment that it finally dawns on him because Izyaan's mouth falls open.

Yasir notices Izyaan staring and follows his gaze over to us. He skims right over Safiya to stare at me. It strikes Yasir faster than Izyaan that I'm sitting in public in a full-on hijab. Even from a distance I can make out Yasir's whole body go rigid. Izyaan turns and meets Yasir's round eyes, a secret message passing between them. I think it's the first time I've ever seen them share a look like that with each other. Like they're thinking the same thing.

I need to know what that thing is.

Without warning Safiya, I rise to my feet and start walking over there.

"Hey, where are you going?" Safiya exclaims, but I'm on autopilot gliding around tables, chairs, and people.

Izyaan and Yasir watch me approach as if in slow motion, wearing twin expressions of uneasiness. The others are completely unaware until I'm right beside their table, and at that point, they all freeze in the middle of whatever they're doing to gape at me. For a long, long while, none of them make a single sound.

"Hi," I say to Izyaan, ignoring the others.

"Hey," Izyaan replies succinctly, his eyes never leaving my head. I wish I could read his mind. All that's giving him away is the slight droop of his mouth in one corner. The palms of my hands start to get clammy. I know it's a sudden change, but is he really *that* shocked by me wearing hijab?

"What's the matter? Cat got your tongues?" Safiya materializes in my periphery with her hands on her hips. Her voice is a warning. *Say one mean thing to Ainy and I'll flip your table upside down.*

Still nothing. Yasir can't seem to decide where to look. I momentarily catch his gaze and smirk, making color rise into his cheeks. The upper hand is finally mine now and he knows it. The others haven't made a single snide remark, which is probably a record. Inside, I breathe a sigh of relief. It actually worked! For the first time all summer, I feel respected. Free.

And a little bold. "Yasir, does your dad's office still have free snacks?" I ask. Safiya stares at me incredulously, but Yasir blanches. He averts his gaze like he wants me to go the heck away. But my question snaps the others out of their trance and Abdul finally digs up his voice.

"Well, I think this is your sign to give up on Ainy, Yasir," he says. "All yours, Izzy. You don't care about looks that much anyway."

His words send a shock wave through me. I clench and unclench my hands at my sides. *Don't react, Ainy. Don't let him get to you.* I wanted this. I wanted Yasir to be less attracted to me, but . . . it *hurt* to hear Abdul say that out loud.

"You little—!"

I hold a hand up to keep Safiya from having a go at Abdul. Instinctively, I glance over at Izyaan. He's staring down at his shoes quietly, his skin red from his neck to his hairline. If he's planning on standing up for me, he sure is taking his sweet time. But then I realize he isn't. He also isn't telling Abdul off for the rude comment. The truth slaps me across the face. He *agrees* with Abdul. I can't believe it. I didn't expect this from *him*. I can't believe I thought he was one of the nice ones, that he might actually like me, but he doesn't care enough to stop the others from making fun of me. The humiliation zaps me to my core. I can't remember the last time I ever felt so small.

I take a deep breath and remind myself that I'm officially off the hook where Yasir's concerned, and that's all that matters. Who cares what Izyaan and the others think? Now I can go out with Safiya and work at Naseerah's Almari without interruption for the rest of the summer. I can finally focus on the bridesmaid dress designs.

"Let's go, Safiya," I say, taking her hand in mine. "We've got better things to do."

We pay for our lunch and cut through the crosswalk back to my mom's store. I never once turn back, but I'd be lying if I said Abdul's words and Izyaan not defending me didn't get under my skin.

I check my appearance in a store window as we pass. For so long, I was nervous but excited about trying out the hijab. Now I don't know if I like the reflection of the girl staring back at me.

CHAPTER 19

Bajjo and Amma are gathered around the computer, getting a feel for the number of orders due within the next week, when I return to the store. Safiya went home, but not before hugging me tightly and telling me that she's proud of me, boys can kick rocks, and to text her if I need anything.

Amma and Bajjo both do a double take when they see me. I'm still wearing Safiya's hijab. My plan with Yasir worked, so there's no point in taking it off if I'm going to stick with it from now on. I was going to have to surprise them sooner or later. Slowly, everyone in my life is going to find out. It's part of my image now.

Amma pulls herself together and her eyes crinkle into a smile. "Did you have a nice lunch?"

"Yep," I say, even though I didn't actually eat anything.

"Good to hear it." Amma isn't reacting the way that I thought at all. The same way as when Bajjo took her hijab off. It's as if nothing is out of the ordinary. I'm a little relieved she isn't grilling me. Bajjo's eyes, on the other hand, are flinty as she regards me.

"I'm going to head out for a dentist appointment," says Amma. "It's long overdue. I trust you two can handle things here while I'm gone." Amma slings her purse over her purple abaya and passes a look between me and Bajjo, reading the tension in the room. If I didn't know any better, I'd say she was silently giving us a warning to behave. "I'll be back soon, in shaa Allah."

Amma's gone for all of five seconds before Bajjo takes a crack at me. "What do you think you're doing?" she demands when I come around to sit behind the counter at my usual spot.

Anger balloons inside me, but I pretend like I didn't hear her. Bajjo has no right prying into my business when she's been keeping secrets and ignoring me for weeks.

"Ainy, I asked you—"

The front door sweeps open at that point, the little bells over the threshold clanging louder than usual as a blustery-faced Gabina Auntie walks in. My heart withers. Oof, she does *not* look happy.

"Where is Naseerah?" Gabina Auntie says without so much as a salaam.

"Amma went out. She'll be back in an hour or so," Bajjo says smoothly. "How can we—?"

"I'll tell you what, ladies," Gabina Auntie interjects. She swings her head at me and spots of color rise on her cheeks. "I think your mother is a very reputable and honest businesswoman. I admire what she has built. However, I cannot say the same for the daughters that she is raising." She stops for a split second to catch her breath. In that time, both Bajjo and I have gone stiff.

"I just saw Ainy and Safiya talking to Yasir and his friends. This is the second time I have seen those girls hanging around the boys for no reason. It would be a great shame if I decided not to praise to people where the bridesmaids got their dresses from because the designer's girls don't know how to behave themselves." Gabina Auntie points a bony finger at Bajjo. "As the older sister, you should have been keeping a close eye on your sister on Saturday instead of frolicking around with your friends. Did you see how close Ainy got with the boys that day? Completely unacceptable. I was shocked. Apparently, this is not the first time either. I hear Ainy is always around Yasir and his friends."

You mean they're *always forcing their way into* my *space!* I want to shriek.

"And I have to wonder *why*," Gabina Auntie bulldozes on. "Surely, it's not because Ambreen's son hangs out with them as well? I've been paying attention to their little *friendship.*"

My blood freezes and the room spins. How—?

Yasir. How else could she know? He ratted me out to his own mom! He knows how scared everyone is of her. That she's a big gossip. I'm speechless. Why would Yasir do that? Was he getting back at me for rejecting him? For liking Izyaan over him?

"You are young, and I understand that. But given that you've evidently made the decision to become a hijabi, I suggest you stop making a mockery out of it by physically presenting yourself as a good Muslim girl while not living up to the values it embodies. I was going to bring this matter to Naseerah and Ambreen pronto. They have a right to know what their children are doing directly under their noses. But since Naseerah isn't here, I'm willing to give you another chance. I don't want to see or hear about Ainy going near my son and his friends again."

With that, Gabina Auntie spins on her heel and marches out of the store. The bells ring in her wake, leaving me and Bajjo standing rooted to the spot. It doesn't take long for Bajjo to blow up. She curses so loudly into the empty storefront that I flinch.

"That evil witch! Who does she think she is, meddling in our lives? The morality police?" Bajjo whirls on me. "Is what she said true? Are you really hanging around Yasir and his friends now?"

"No!" I explode. "Gabina Auntie has it all wrong. I'm not doing anything wrong." I'm a good kid.

"Ainy, talk to me," Bajjo presses. "What is going on? You haven't been acting like yourself."

"Speak for yourself. Can't believe you even notice or remember that I exist," I say.

Bajjo gives me an intense look. "Do those boys have anything to do with why you're wearing the hijab now?"

My mouth flops open and closed like a confused fish. Bajjo's on point, but I'm offended that *that's* the first conclusion she came to. Still, it's an opening. A big piece of me wants to confide in Bajjo the way I would have before everything between us went down the drain.

"First, you tell me why you suddenly decided to stop being a hijabi," I say.

Bajjo bites her lip, and judging by the hesitant look on her face, I know she's not going to give me a straight answer. Something inside me tears open in that moment. My own sister doesn't trust me anymore to be herself around me, so why should I trust her? I gave her a chance to be honest with me, to come clean, and she's not taking it. That tells me everything I need to know about who's on my side.

The rage returns and this time I don't quell it. "You're a huge disappointment, you know," I say. "I can't believe you gave up so easily. But I didn't need your help after all. I found the strength to be a hijabi all by myself, no thanks to you. You were probably already thinking of taking it off and that's why you never liked the thought of me starting. Because it would make you look bad in front of everyone and you don't like to be anything but perfect."

Bajjo's face distorts in shock. For a minute, my sister looks as if she's going to cry or scream or both. But instead, she turns her head, her ponytail cutting through the air behind her like a whip. "If that's what you believe, Ainy, then suit yourself." Then she disappears into the back room, the door slamming firmly shut between us like a brick wall.

CHAPTER 20

Bajjo and I are still giving each other the cold shoulder when we go for our monthly youth halaqah—a religious gathering or meeting to study Islam—at the masjid on Friday evening. Except now the tension is extra thick. Bajjo, Amarah, Safiya, Izyaan, and I carpooled, and Amarah and Safiya are definitely noticing the chill in the air, but neither of them breaks the ice.

The halaqah takes place in one of the classrooms on the masjid's third floor where the Islamic school is. There are always lots of events taking place on Fridays, especially over the summer. Even though the door is closed, I can hear footsteps and laughter and chitchat over Sister Ala and Brother Nuh's honey-sleek voices as they lecture us from behind their respective podiums at the front of the room. Tonight's topic is about how we can all grow closer to Allah by making small changes in our everyday lives.

What those small changes are, I couldn't tell you, because I'm paying more attention to the back of Bajjo's head than our teachers. It's strange to see her in a hijab again. Sister Ala asks a question that pulls me out of my thoughts for a millisecond before I go right back to spacing out. Guilt flickers in my chest. I've been so caught up in, well, everything else this summer that I haven't been spending a lot of time on *this* part of my life. The part that Abu says should always matter the most. Even now, all I can concentrate on is the panic coursing through me because I'm out of time. Amma's expecting the bridesmaid dress designs from me by today, but I couldn't come up with anything. Literally, I had four weeks and nothing came out of it. The thought of facing Amma with the embarrassing truth when we go home is too much to bear.

When the session is over, Bajjo, Amarah, Safiya, and I take the stairs down to the masjid's brightly lit café while Izyaan strays off with his friends. There's already a crowd when we enter. We snag a spot in line behind some other teen girls whose faces are kind of familiar. I see them around the masjid from time to time. Bajjo and

Amarah probably know them better because they run in the same circle, but Bajjo's not her usual talkative self. Her eyes are glued to the floor like she doesn't want anyone to see her. My brow furrows.

"Do you want me to send you my notes?" Safiya asks, flipping the pages of her notebook filled with her handwriting. I can tell she knows I wasn't paying attention today.

"Sure," I say distractedly, catching how one of the girls in front of us—the one with superthick eyeliner—looks over her shoulder at Bajjo with a sneer as Bajjo lifts her hijab from the back to fix her ponytail.

The girl leans in to whisper to her friend in a voice that's definitely meant to be heard. "Don't see why she bothers to pretend anymore when she's just going to treat it like a game."

Bajjo's hands go still on the back of her neck, the shape of her shoulders tight as a rope. Even Safiya looks up at the older girls with a quizzical expression.

"Some people have no respect," her friend murmurs back. "At least she has *some* shame."

"Mind your own business, Alana," Amarah barks. "The only one with no shame here is you. Talking behind someone's back with them standing right here. As if turning up your nose at her for weeks for a decision that had nothing to do with you wasn't bad enough."

Understanding lights my brain. Bajjo's friends have been freezing her out because she took her hijab off? I look to Bajjo. She's still staring at her shoes like she's wishing the floor would swallow her up.

Their comments sound like a remixed version of what Gabina Auntie said to me a few days ago. Heat crawls up my neck when I recall how Gabina Auntie basically accused me of not being good enough to wear the hijab. That's exactly what this girl is doing to Bajjo. It feels like she's calling me out, too. "Of course you're defending her," Alana with the eyeliner says. "Takes a phony to know one."

"What are you, the haram police? You're going to stand here, inside a masjid no less, and talk down to us? Wow, Alana. You're a shining citizen. I forgot nobody is allowed to make mistakes or change their mind in life except for you," says Amarah.

I'm hoping this is the point when Bajjo will speak up. But she's reverted to a five-year-old kid afraid to stand up to her bullies. Who is this? My sister would never let anyone walk all over her like that! By now she would've burned Alana and her friend so bad they wouldn't dare insult her again.

Safiya pushes her way forward to stand next to Amarah and in front of Bajjo with enough vigor to capsize someone twice her size. "Amarah's right. Quit being so mean. You don't get to judge anyone."

Alana doesn't look happy about being sassed by a twelve-year-old. A twelve-year-old who isn't *me*.

I should've been the one to defend her first, not Amarah or Safiya. So why didn't I? Why aren't I?

For a brief second, Bajjo lifts her glassy eyes to mine and holds my gaze. And . . . I can't take it. Fine, I don't like that she took the hijab off, but that doesn't mean she deserves to be treated like garbage by these mean girls and their nastiness. It's not fair. It's not right. I can't watch.

I bolt out of the café. I think Safiya shouts my name, but I don't stop until I make a sharp turn down the long hallway and topple into a chair holding the gym's door ajar. The sound of squeaking sneakers and a dribbling basketball can't drown out Alana's derisive voice inside my head. *Takes a phony to know one.* I swallow hard. I called Bajjo a disappointment a few days ago for the same reason. Oh my God, how did that make me any better than Alana? Why couldn't I see how wrong that was before?

"I'll get it!" someone calls from the gym at the exact same time that a basketball rolls right out the open door and thuds against my leg. Mechanically, I bend down to pick it up, but I'm only halfway when Yasir comes bounding out of the gym with sweat gleaming on his forehead and underneath the armpits of his T-shirt. For the first time in weeks, the sight of his face doesn't irk me. I'm safe from him now that I'm a hijabi.

Yasir glances at me. "You lose, Mustafa!" he yells over his shoulder. He swings to the side so that the others can see me hovering outside the gym. Izyaan's with them. He pauses mid-stride, a worried look filling the lines of his face.

"Proves nothing. We're in a masjid," Mustafa hollers back.

Yasir spins back to me, smirking. "We made a bet."

Don't take the bait.

I take it. "What kind of bet?" I ask. The feeling of invisibility and armor strength falls away from me.

"How long you'll last wearing that." Yasir nods at my head, but he might as well have slapped me across the face because I recoil anyway. "Mustafa said two days. Abdul and Shezi said a week. I said you're a Goody Two-shoes, so at least a month. Izyaan didn't really care. Sooner or later, though, we all agree it's just a phase." Yasir smiles at me, but it looks deranged. "If your perfect sister gave up, there's no way you're gonna stick with it."

My stomach turns over and it feels like I'm gonna puke. It's never going to end. The hijab was supposed to be deflecting attention from me, the way it's meant to! What was the point in wearing it if it's not going to make me feel safe from unwanted attention?

My eyes widen as the thought crosses my mind. They're right. I'm not strong enough and they know it. Already I'm doubting myself and all it took was one jab at me. Did Bajjo get this when she was a hijabi, too? No wonder she buckled under all the pressure. But if I take it off, then how am I going to get these boys to leave me alone? I'm out of options.

"I better not have heard you say what I think you just did," a dangerously low voice says from behind me. Bajjo, Amarah, and Safiya have found me. Bajjo's got dagger eyes locked on Yasir like she wants to crush him into a ball and slam-dunk him into the nearest hoop.

They heard everything.

CHAPTER 21

Bajjo takes a step toward Yasir with her hands balled into fists. A few minutes ago, she was hesitant in front of Alana, but she's not showing any signs of being a weakling here.

"How dare you treat Ainy like that," Bajjo says coldly.

Yasir flinches like he can feel the heat of Bajjo's blazing eyes. His face clenches with, not fear exactly, but he's for sure intimidated. Izyaan's eyes fall on Amarah and he curls in on himself at the accusing look in his older sister's eyes.

"Are you making fun of my little sister, kid?" Bajjo can't control the shake in her voice. "What gives you the right to talk to her—to talk to *any* girl—like that?"

"Bajjo. Don't." My voice scrapes up my throat.

Time seems to both fly and crawl. I can't keep the embarrassment off my face. I thought I was done feeling like I'm doing something wrong to make myself a target, but now the same old guilt washes over me. I wish more than anything that Bajjo, Safiya, and Amarah hadn't come after me and hadn't heard the boys treat me like a worm. The way I *let* them treat me, I realize with a jolt. Like how Bajjo let Alana walk all over her, even though Bajjo didn't do anything to deserve it.

"We were just having some fun," Yasir says. His voice gets picked up and bounced around the gym. "Lighten up."

"You call insulting someone fun?" Bajjo asks in a low tremble. "I bet no one's ever taught you how to respect girls. Not with parents like yours."

"Bajjo."

It isn't the anger spiking on Yasir's face that makes gooseflesh rise on my arms, but that's not good news either. It's the brief hurt that flashes across Amarah's and Izyaan's expressions in reaction to Bajjo offending their relatives. I know they don't disagree with her, but they aren't going to speak badly about them either. And while Gabina Auntie might be a sore spot for Yasir, I also know now that he'll tell his mom some warped version of what actually happened to make him look like the victim.

Anything Bajjo says in the heat of the moment here is fair game to get back to Gabina Auntie's ears. We can't afford to have Gabina Auntie turn against us. Amma's business is on the line. And who's to say Amarah and Izyaan won't blab to Sister Ambreen about what Bajjo said? Next thing we know, we're on the streets for stirring up problems in their family. And after everything they've done for us.

The air in the gym is charged. Abdul, Shezi, and Mustafa wait silently, their gazes fixed on Yasir's back. They're not going to get their hands dirty when they can throw their leader under the bus. *Some friends.*

"It's just a game to you, isn't it?" *Oh my God, Bajjo, just let it go!* "You know no one's going to force you to do anything. That society is always going to let you off the hook. Meanwhile, we never hear the end of it. 'Don't wear the hijab.' 'Wear the hijab.' 'No, not like that.' 'Not pious enough.' 'Too extreme.' 'What will the boys think?' I'll tell you what you should think. *Nothing!*" Bajjo jabs a finger in his direction. "You don't get a say in what we do or don't wear and you never will! Nothing gives you the right to harass us. And you roaches don't get to *take bets* on the matter."

I don't dare blink or move, afraid of missing a single moment. Except this is not like when you're at the movies holding your pee because you don't want to miss out on an exciting scene. I'd give any excuse to flee this gym right now. Safiya's gaping at me like she's never seen me before, and I can see all her thoughts swirling behind her eyes. Putting things together.

"Stay away from Ainy," Bajjo warns through bared teeth. "If I see any of you come near her again, you are going to seriously regret it. Let's go, Ainy."

Not left with much of a choice, I scuttle after her with my head ducked down.

"You have a lot of explaining to do later," I hear Amarah snipe as she drags Izyaan out of the gym by his shirt collar. If I had to guess, he's going to get an earful at home. Good. He deserves it. He's no better than the rest of them.

I follow Bajjo, Amarah, Izyaan, and Safiya out into the masjid's parking lot. A light, humid drizzle is hanging in the air. Only Izyaan gets into Amarah's car right away. Bajjo spins on her heel and leans against the trunk, pegging me with X-ray eyes.

"How long has this been going on?" Bajjo demands.

"Ainy," Amarah says gently when I squeeze my eyes shut. "Tell us."

"They were just making fun of my hijab," I say meekly.

"Why didn't you tell them to shove off?" Bajjo exclaims. "That's how it always starts! This obsession with controlling our bodies!"

"What about you?" I counter. "I didn't see you fight back in the café when Alana dragged you through the mud!"

Bajjo grimaces. "I've been dealing with people's attitudes for the last four years. You've only dealt with it for a few days! You need to have thicker skin than that if you truly want to be a hijabi. That's exactly what I've been trying to tell you! What those boys did back there is just the tip of the iceberg."

"She's right, Ainy," Safiya says, wrapping her hand around my arm. "Maybe you weren't as ready as you thought you were to do this."

I snatch my arm back from her, her words carrying the weight of betrayal. I'm so sick of being put down like a little kid who's not ready to take on hard things. Everyone always acts like they know more than me, and I'm so over it.

"Not everyone can be like you," I lash out at Safiya. "Stop acting like being strong is a piece of cake. You can barely handle being around a baby without turning into one yourself."

I realize a beat too late what I said when Safiya drops her hand with a wounded expression.

"Wait, I didn't mean—"

But Safiya backs out of my reach, hugging her arms to her chest like she's trying to hold herself together. "I'm gonna call my mom to come pick me up," she says.

"Safiya—" I plead, my heart stuck in my throat.

Safiya turns around and runs through the mist back inside the masjid, but not right before we all hear her burst into tears.

Bajjo sags against Amarah's car, shaking her head. "I sense there's a lot more to the story than you're letting on. We can talk at home."

"What if I don't want to?" I ask stubbornly.

Bajjo holds the back seat door open for me. "Let's see what Amma has to say when I tell her what happened."

CHAPTER 22

I beg Bajjo the whole way home not to tell Amma, but she acts like she can't hear me. Amarah keeps her eyes trained on the road, knuckles white on the steering wheel as she drives at a dead crawl. Outside, the rain is coming down sideways now. When we make it to the Khalids' driveway in one piece, Amarah kills the engine and sits back.

Bajjo unbuckles her seat belt exasperatedly and looks over at Amarah. "Talk later?"

"Oh, you bet," says Amarah. She glares into the rearview mirror at Izyaan, only the set of her jaw hinting at how mad she is.

Bajjo and I sprint around the back of the house in the rain until we're standing underneath the Khalids' deck. A faint light illuminates the thin curtains hanging over the sliding glass doors leading to the basement.

I block the entrance, taking one last stab at stopping Bajjo from barging in there and ruining everything. "Bajjo, if Amma finds out what happened, she's going to tell Gabina Auntie." I don't have to explain to her why that would be disastrous. She knows which one of them has more influence and the power to ruin our lives. "Abu told me to take care of you guys. I can handle Yasir. It's not a big deal."

Bajjo stares at me hard. "I assure you, Ainy, this is not what Abu meant. As for Amma confronting Gabina Auntie about how Yasir treated you"—she swipes me to the side—"I'm counting on it. Trust me. This is for your own good."

Before I can argue further, she's inside.

"Asalamualaikum," Amma says. She's sitting at the dining table with her phone and cup of chai, her dark hair twisted up and secured with a claw clip. In the living room, Kashif's got his back to us. He's got his headphones on, talking to a friend as they game.

Amma laughs at our disheveled appearance. "Wow, it's really coming down out there. How was—?"

"Amma, we need to talk," Bajjo says without preamble. "Actually, Ainy has something she needs to tell you."

Amma's smile fades as she regards us. "Okay. What is it?"

The last couple of weeks haven't felt right at all. Like a dress with a broken zipper that doesn't fit anymore. I can't let Bajjo do this. It's going to ruin everything. But if I don't spill, she will. It might as well be me. At least I can make it sound like Bajjo's exaggerating. Then maybe Amma won't do anything extreme to get on Gabina Auntie's bad side.

"It's nothing," I say. "Yasir—you know, Gabina Auntie's son—he and his friends were making fun of me."

"About what?" Amma prods.

I cross my ankles uncomfortably. "My hijab. But that's normal, right? Boys are just like that."

"Who in their right mind told you *that*?" Bajjo shrieks. "That is not normal!"

"But Aaira Auntie and Lubna Auntie said at the exhibition that it is normal! That a lot of boys don't want to marry a hijabi because it makes them look less pretty!"

Silence. Only the sound of rain outside cuts through the heaviness. Sweat springs up on my forehead at my mistake. I try to think of a way to backpedal, but nothing sounds convincing.

Amma's hand is deathly still on her mug. "You don't honestly believe what those women said? And if you do, why would you need to make yourself look less pretty?"

I flail with a comeback. "I don't. I wanted to. Wear the hijab, I mean. For a long time. You guys know that."

"Yes, but I always thought you would come to me or Kulsoom when you were ready," says Amma. She sounds sad that I left them out. "I was waiting to see if you would come and talk to me about your decision."

My chest tightens. If Amma only knew how much I wanted to pour my heart out to her, but I couldn't risk endangering the business.

"Uh. Yeah, I—it was . . . time. I'm twelve. I get my period."

Bajjo's not buying it. "If you'd told me that at the beginning of the summer, I would've believed you. But now?" Bajjo squints at me with one of her I-can-see-right-through-your-lies looks. "What aren't you telling us? There's something fishy going on here, Ainy. I know you. I know how important becoming a hijabi was for you. You wanted to do it at the right time, the right way. The fact that you jumped into it was a huge red flag."

"I don't get why you won't encourage me instead of always trying to get me to not wear hijab!" I complain. "Just because you don't anymore—"

"Me taking the hijab off was not about *you*, Ainy. And stop trying to change the subject. Don't try to turn all of this around on me."

My tongue feels thick and my insides jumbled. For weeks, I couldn't talk to Amma because she was always so stressed and busy. Couldn't confide in Bajjo because she was battling some invisible fight she didn't want me to know about. Couldn't share with Abu because of him dealing with Dadi's sickness. Or Safiya because I didn't want to look weak next to her strength and bravery.

But I didn't ask Yasir and his friends to target me day after day either. And I didn't realize until now how lonely and scared I've been all this time. For once, I want to stop feeling like a sitting duck. I want someone to protect me and not care about the consequences even though it's selfish. For my life to go back to the way it was before. All I wanted was to work at Amma's store and design clothes. To help my family. I don't want to deal with this by myself anymore.

And that's what finally drags the truth out of me. "Yasir likes me and he hasn't left me alone ever since school ended."

I start from the beginning, telling Amma and Bajjo everything that's happened since my first day working at Naseerah's Almari. Yasir following me around even after I kept telling him no. Abdul, Shezi, and Mustafa's involvement. My phone call with Abu. Gabina Auntie. The bridesmaid dresses. The horrible comments I read online. My design block. My feelings for Izyaan. And finally, the real reason why I started hijab after asking for Safiya's help. My throat threatens to strangle my words, but I push through until I reach the end.

"I didn't want you guys to make a big deal out of it," I say to Amma and Bajjo's appalled expressions.

"Ainy, it is a big deal!" Bajjo says, looking distraught. "You should've told us all of this was happening! You should've told *me* at least. I don't get why you didn't come to me in the first place."

"I tried!" I make a half-sob, half-choking sound. "But then you started avoiding me and turned into a completely different person! You wouldn't tell me what's going on with *you*! I didn't know if I could trust you anymore."

At that, Bajjo seems to lose her balance. She falls into the chair next to Amma, and turns to face me with glistening eyes. "I didn't know you took me not being a hijabi anymore so hard. I mean, I kind of knew you would, but not this much."

"I looked up to you more than anyone," I say.

"I know, Ainy. That's why I couldn't talk to you about it. You had these same expectations of me that everyone else had. To be a star at everything. But I'm just a regular person and I was so sick of everyone judging me if I didn't live up to some impossible standard." Bajjo lets out a ragged breath. "I was scrutinized more by everybody *because* I was a hijabi. It felt like I was never allowed to make mistakes. Expected to be perfect. It's bad enough when others do it, but when your own people do it, too?"

Bajjo stares down at her lap, digging her nails into the fabric of her jumpsuit, then looks back up at me. "You know what happened the day you started working at the store? While you and Safiya were out, a regular customer came in for something, and while she and I were talking, she straight-up asked me when I'm going to start covering my face, too. I have nothing against niqab, obviously. And I get that she probably didn't mean anything by it, but I took that question so *personally*. People already hold me to a different standard for covering my hair. How much worse would it get if I wore niqab, too? I'm always 'representing' instead of being treated like a human being. Trust me. Taking the hijab off wasn't a decision I made overnight. Everything started to get to me slowly over time, and I started to lose sight of why I did hijab in the first place. I guess that day was a breaking point for me. Amma knows. I told her before I started going outside without it."

That explains why Amma never questioned Bajjo. She already had the insider scoop. But if people thought *Bajjo* wasn't good enough, then who am I to think I'm any better? Hearing my sister speak her mind out loud now, I start to wonder if I *did* expect too much from her. Maybe I was being too hard on myself, too.

"I had no idea," I say. "I used to think you were invincible *because* of your hijab." A tear trickles down my cheek. "What am I doing wrong? How come I don't feel anything special when I wear hijab? I thought it would make me a better Muslim, but nothing changed."

"Beta," Amma says gently. She gets up and comes over to bend down in front of me, taking my hands in her calloused ones. "First of all, hijab is not something you earn. It's not a prize." She turns to Bajjo and pulls her closer, too. "And it's not supposed to be a burden, either.

The whole purpose of our faith is not to be 'good enough' for something. Wearing hijab should be for one reason and one reason only." She taps me under my chin, making me look her in the eyes. "We wear it to please Allah. It's the only intention that will stick because everyone else in the world will let you down. But He won't. No matter how many times you fall down. Hijab is first and foremost an act of love and worship. It is not a means to a spiritual end. If you treat hijab like an accessory or a trend . . . well. Aren't trends temporary? Don't they go out of style? Is that how you want your relationship with Allah to be?"

"But I'm not wearing it for Allah," I admit softly. "I'm not even sure I'm wearing it because I want to right now. I just wanted Yasir and those boys to leave me alone."

Amma presses her forehead to mine, and it's only then that I notice she's crying. "God, I feel terrible," she says. "I can't believe I've been so busy that I didn't even pay attention to what's been going on with my own daughter."

"Don't feel bad, Amma," I say. "You're making your dreams come true. That's huge. And you're working extra hard while Abu's away. For us. That's kind of the reason why I didn't want to tell you about Yasir. At least until Gabina Auntie's order was done. I didn't want her to cancel the bridesmaid dresses, because I know it's a big and important order."

"No amount of money is worth my child's well-being. Those boys cannot do and say whatever they want. That's sexual harassment, and the longer we let it go on, the more they're going to think that no one will hold them accountable for their actions."

"Ainy," says Bajjo. "Think about it. You put the hijab *on* because boys were bothering you, but some girls take it *off* for the same reason. What does that tell you? You are not the problem. They are. They choose to behave like that."

You are not the problem. I let loose a breath I didn't know I'd been holding. All this time, I was convinced it was my fault for drawing too much attention to myself.

"And that's something I remind Kashif of often," Amma says, waving her hand over to where Kashif's fixated on his game. "It doesn't matter how a woman dresses. You are to always respect her. Unfortunately, bad eggs are everywhere. That's just the nature of this dunya. But I promise you, not all boys are like Yasir and his friends." Amma smiles. "In fact, when I first married your abu, I didn't used to be a hijabi or a niqabi. I didn't start until after I moved to the US. But your abu was my biggest supporter, even when my whole family was against it. Why do you think my sister in Texas wants nothing to do with me?" Amma rolls her eyes, but I can tell it really hurts her. "Anyway, the point is, do not ever feel like you have to change yourself for anyone. Your own self-respect is more important. Hijab itself isn't going to force anyone to respect you. You have to do that by standing up for yourself."

That's when it hits me. When it came to my decision about wearing the hijab, Bajjo taking hers off shouldn't have mattered. How those rowdy boys were treating me, with or without it, shouldn't have mattered. I shouldn't have even cared about what Izyaan would think. I should've only cared about what I wanted and my own relationship with Allah, which, clearly, needs a lot of work.

"You guys make everything look so easy," I huff. "It's not fair."

"Amma sure does," Bajjo adds.

"Oh, do I?" Amma laughs, and Bajjo and I can't help but join in.

Bajjo comes over and hugs me. "I'm sorry I let you down and for being a crappy sister."

I bury my face in her shirt. "Me too. I'm sorry for all the mean things I said to you." Without Amma and Bajjo,

I was stumbling through the dark hoping I didn't trip over my own feet. Finally, there's a light and I can see again.

The warm, tingly feeling's only fleeting, though, because I remember one more problem.

"So, I have a confession to make about the bridesmaid dresses . . ."

CHAPTER 23

"My eyes!" I shield my face from the monstrosity before me.

"That is the ugliest thing I've ever seen," Bajjo comments, clutching her hand to her chest.

"Hey now, let's be nice," Amma says with mock offense. "No, you're right. It's hideous. That's why I have it all locked up in here."

Bajjo, Amma, and I are gathered in Amma's tiny bedroom, where she's unleashed half a dozen storage containers containing a multitude of clothes I have zero memory of her ever making. Some of them are half-finished, but most don't deserve to see the light of day without a hazard label. Even *tacky* seems too nice a word to describe them.

"Where did all of these come from anyway?" I ask, picking up a pink kameez thing that looks like a flamingo threw up a ton of little mirrors on itself. I toss it back onto the bed with a choking sound.

"My failures. Or rather, my missteps. Some are ones that customers changed their minds about, so I keep them in case they come in handy in the future. It's taken me years to be able to do things right on the first try," says Amma.

"Hard to believe coming from you," Bajjo comments, flopping on top of the bed, scattering clothes left and right. "None of your clients would be caught dead in one of these."

"We all make mistakes." Amma looks at me with warm eyes. I finally came clean to her and Bajjo about my designer's block and how I haven't been able to think of anything for the bridesmaid dresses.

"I'm sorry I didn't tell you sooner, Amma," I said sheepishly. "I didn't want you to think I was a bad designer."

Amma wasn't upset at all. "If you'd been struggling, all you needed to do was ask for my help. I think you have a natural knack for designing, but sometimes we all need a little morale boost." Then she told me and Bajjo to follow her.

Amma nudges me with her leg. "You're not the only one who suffers from designer's block. Sometimes I burn myself out to the point where I can't even pick up a pencil or sewing needle anymore. So, you know what I do to get myself through it?" Amma picks up a handful of clothes and tosses them in the air like confetti. "I make horrible clothes! On purpose! I let go of all my perfectionism and create with no boundaries. It frees my mind and lets me explore new ideas without putting too much pressure on myself."

"That explains the Frankenstein dresses," Bajjo laughs. "Your mind sure took a long rest."

Amma winks at us. "A rested mind is a powerful mind when it's ready to get back on its grind."

"They're not all hideous," I say. I pull out a poofy-sleeved blouse paired with a cheap tulle skirt and hold it against my body. Okay, it *is* hideous, but I pretend for five seconds that it's not. I spin in a circle on one foot and bat my eyelashes at Amma and Bajjo. "I'd wear this to a princess ball."

"Sure. If you're planning on scaring Prince Charming out of there screaming at the top of his lungs," Bajjo says, and Amma bursts out laughing. Bajjo digs through the boxes and unfolds a blue lehenga that looks decent at first glance, except . . .

Bajjo peeks at us through the hundreds of little holes in the unlined netting. "Peekaboo!"

Amma scratches her head. "I can't even remember where that's from."

"The color's pretty," I note. Despite everything here being a reject, the designer in me can't help but keep exploring. Even Bajjo sits with me, sifting through dozens of styles that are out of fashion now like they're treasure finds. And I can feel it. My mind whirring. That old itch to create rekindling inside me as I scour the containers' contents.

My eyes catch on a floral patchwork border and I reach for it. Turns out it's actually the hemline of what can only be described as a long cardigan, except it's made from navy-blue georgette fabric and embellished with very subtle sequins and a beaded string that can be tied right below the chest.

"Uh, Amma?" I ask. "Did you put this in here by accident?"

Amma looks up from where she's folding and packing away stuff we've already ditched. "Oh, that old thing. It used to be one of my abayas. I loved the color, so I was trying to salvage it by giving it a new look, but ended up goofing up the size and it became too short for me."

"I think it'll fit Bajjo." I pass it to my sister. "Here, try it on."

Bajjo stands up and gives the cardigan a good shaking out before pulling the sleeves on. I was right. It fits her perfectly. "You look amazing!" Bajjo spins. The coat fans out around her, the sequins twinkling like little stars. It even suits the wide-legged jumpsuit Bajjo's got on.

"I'm stealing this!" Bajjo announces, but I don't hear her because my heart is suddenly pounding. An image forms in my mind's eye. A beautiful outfit that combines a jumpsuit with a more traditional-looking long coat.

"That's it!" I exclaim, jumping to my feet.

"What's it?" Bajjo asks, startled by my outburst.

"A jumpsuit! Some of them have pants with wide legs that make them look like a full skirt!"

Amma and Bajjo exchange a confused glance. "Okay . . . ?"

I lunge for Amma's nightstand, where she keeps a notepad and pen. I flip to a blank page and draw on my lap as I keep babbling. "Hear me out. You know how some trousers on Pakistani clothes are made super wide to make them look like a skirt? What if we did that but put them on a one-piece jumpsuit instead? Then we can design a long coat to wear on top for a more formal look.

It'll be like a two-in-one style! Bridesmaids have to do so much. They can put the coat on for the bride's entrance and pictures on the wedding day. Then they can take the coat off when they want to feel more comfortable, like when they're eating. Either way, they'll look fabulous."

I show my hasty scribbles to Amma and Bajjo. My sketch isn't winning me any prizes, but I think they get the gist, especially when Bajjo's face splits into a huge grin. "Modern meets traditional. Genius."

"I love it," Amma says, winking at me. My heart soars somewhere far, far above the clouds and I realize maybe this is what she had intended to happen all along when she showed me her abandoned designs. For the scraps of clothes to punch through my block and inspire me to design again.

I did it.

"I can add a design to the bodice area and sew pearl buttons all the way down the coat," Amma continues. "It shouldn't be that hard. But we're on a bit of a tight sched-ule if we want to deliver these to Gabina on time."

"Three weeks to make eight jumpsuits. We'll help. We can do it." I rally.

Amma pulls me and Bajjo into a hug. "Then we'd bet-ter get started. I'm going to put the final design together

212

and send it to Gabina for approval right away. Once that's cleared, we have a lot of work to do."

I can't contain my excitement. Eight girls are going to be wearing *my* design at a huge wedding. There are going to be pictures all over social media. It's almost as good as a model showing off one of my dresses in a magazine. One day, models *will* wear the clothes I design, and do photo shoots. And maybe Amma and I can achieve that dream together, because if I've learned anything today, it's that I never want to cut my mom or sister out of any part of my life again. The good or the bad. I should've trusted that they'd have my back. About Yasir. About all of it.

Speaking of having someone's back, there's one more person I need to talk to. It's time I told Safiya the whole truth. But after what I said to her outside the masjid, I just hope it's not too late.

CHAPTER 24

Amma told me not to waste any time and to apologize to Safiya right away.

"When we break someone's heart, it's our responsibility to set things right as quickly as possible," she explained. "Allah doesn't like it when people fight."

I'm all for getting my best friend back, especially if it will make Allah happy, too. Amma drives me over to Safiya's during my lunch break the next day after we stop to pick up crepes. Suha Auntie knows I'm coming and she opens the door for me. I can't chicken out now that I'm on their front porch, so I wave to Amma before slipping off my shoes and stepping inside their house.

"Safiya's in her room," Suha Auntie says while a happy Noor tries charming me into picking her up. Suha Auntie squeezes my shoulder encouragingly and I climb the stairs until I'm standing outside Safiya's bedroom at the end of the hallway. From inside, I can hear other voices, like Safiya's watching something. Taking a deep breath, I knock.

"I'm not hungry, Mama!"

"Special delivery," I call back.

Heavy silence.

"They're crepes," I add, more uncertainly. "With Nutella and strawberries. Your favorite."

Still nothing, but the voices on the other side have paused. Progress. I keep talking at the GIRL CAVE sign hanging outside Safiya's door.

"You don't have to come out if you don't want to," I say. "I get it. But I still want you to know that I'm sorry for what I said to you yesterday."

Socked footsteps sound from the other side and I stand up taller out of surprise when Safiya throws the door open, leaning against the doorframe with her arms folded. She's in fuzzy purple pajamas with her curly hair braided down her back. It's Safiya's signature sleepover look and a lump forms in my throat when I remember how long it's been since we had one. I think she was ready to let me have it, but I guess my face is sorry enough that

215

she just steals the take-out boxes out of my hands and flounces back to her bed.

I carefully walk into her room, which is ten times cleaner than mine but just as familiar. I can tell you exactly which drawer Safiya likes to keep all her jewelry, makeup, socks, even underwear in.

"Aren't you supposed to be at work?" Safiya asks, tearing open the plastic wrap of a disposable fork. She doesn't meet my eyes as she unplugs her tablet from its charger and sets it aside.

"I'm on my lunch break," I reply. I'm still standing in the middle of her room like a cat that wandered in. "Look, about yesterday—"

Safiya cuts me off. "If you hated listening to me vent about Noor so much, you could've just said so."

I shake my head. "It's not that, Saf. I swear. It's just—" I sigh, already worn out and I haven't even started to tell her the truth. There's just so much. But Safiya deserves every detail, no matter how much time it takes. "It's a long story."

Safiya finally looks up at me, sucking on the inside of her cheek. Thinking. Then she scoots over to make room for me next to her on the bed. I launch into the story before I'm even sitting down all the way. I leave nothing out because I'm tired of keeping secrets from my best friend. I tell her about everything going on behind the scenes. How Yasir and his friends have been treating me since school ended; why I started avoiding us hanging out; my promise to Abu, Dadi, Izyaan, Bajjo; the bridesmaid dresses and how we needed the money; the mean comments; my designer's block; why I took a chance on the hijab. It's not until everything's tumbling out that I realize this summer has been anything but what we planned it to be. I talk to the backs of my hands most of the time. By the time I'm done, our crepes have gone completely cold. My lunch break is definitely over, but Amma hasn't messaged me.

"That's all," I conclude.

"That's *all*?" Safiya shrieks. I balk when I notice the tears streaking down her cheeks. "Are you serious? I can't believe you didn't tell me sooner! I can't believe I didn't even *notice*! That Yasir! When I get my hands on him, he's finished! The rest of those idiots, too!"

"I don't think Gabina Auntie would appreciate that." I chuckle.

"This isn't funny, Ainy!" Safiya says, shoving me. "Your mom's right. We can't let those guys get away with it anymore."

"I know. I want them to get in trouble, but . . . I finally broke through my designer's block and came up with the perfect bridesmaid dress design. Even Amma agrees it's the one, but I really don't like giving them to Yasir's mom." My relief bursts when reality hits me. "Amma's business might not get the recognition it deserves. Gabina Auntie already doesn't like us. Imagine how much more awful she's gonna be if we tell her about Yasir. She'll probably say that I'm lying. Will it hurt Amma's reputation? What if Sister Ambreen kicks us out of her house?" My voice hitches.

"It's worth it. You can come live with us," Safiya says without missing a beat. "If you have to spend every day with Noor, you'll see how awful it actually is."

"Um, did you forget I have a little brother?" I ask.

"Kashif looks up to you. The same way I do," Safiya admits. I look at her in surprise. "You're a good big sister. Before Noor was born, I was actually excited. I thought I could be like you. But then"—Safiya shrugs—"things were different. Sometimes I wish she wasn't even born. I know it sounds bad, but my parents are always so busy. When you didn't want to spend time with me anymore, it felt like I was losing you, too. I didn't want to be in the house anymore. I don't know how to be a big sister. Man, you had all this crap going on in your life and I was complaining about poopy diapers?"

I laugh, more because a little baby made big, brave Safiya all insecure. Oh, how the tables did turn. "Poopy diapers are terrifying. I don't blame you. You're not a bad sister, Safiya. In fact, I bet when Noor grows up, you're going to be her best friend."

"You think so?"

I nod, linking my fingers with hers. "You've been the world's best sister this whole time. To me. I'm sorry I haven't been the same."

"Shut up, Ainy Zain. I'm done crying."

"Well, now we know who Noor's been taking lessons from."

Safiya slams me with her pillow and I fall on the floor laughing. My chest feels lighter suddenly. "But seriously, I'm sorry I called you a baby yesterday. You're not a baby. I was feeling down about myself, and I took it out on you. I was a jerk."

Safiya dangles her foot over the edge of the bed and pokes my shoulder. "Apology accepted."

I sit up on my elbows and regard Safiya. "You know, you should tell your parents how you feel about them shutting you out for Noor all the time. Maybe they don't realize how much it's hurting you." I grin. "Sometimes it helps to share our problems. At least they would know."

"Yeah." Safiya sighs. "You're probably right."

"I can be there when you talk to them. For moral support."

"When?" asks Safiya. "You're going to be busier than ever helping your mom make the bridesmaid dresses."

"Maybe we can finally have one of our sleepovers?" I ask hopefully. "I miss them. I don't think Amma will say no to me spending one night at your place, especially on my day off."

Safiya's face lights up. "That would be amazing. And I can help you guys with the bridesmaid dresses. That means cheer you on because I can't sew to save my life. But Kashif and I can make sure you have plenty of brownies on hand."

The image makes me feel all warm and fuzzy inside until Safiya asks, "What are you going to do about Yasir? Gabina Auntie's gotta know."

My hearts drags low. The idea of facing Gabina Auntie with the truth scares me. But then I think about what Amma said about not letting bad behavior slide. I'm just one person. One voice. But one person is better than nobody. I can make some kind of difference. And what I know for sure now is that I don't have to do it alone.

My lips twitch into an almost smile. For the first time all summer, I feel like I have the power to take Yasir down now that Amma and Bajjo and Safiya are on my side. I'm not going to hide anymore. Whatever happens happens, but at least I'll know that I stood up for myself.

"I'm going to do what I should've done a long time ago," I say.

CHAPTER 25

Delivery day for the big order arrives in the blink of an eye. One minute we're at Naseerah's Almari running back and forth all day, going straight home after to gather materials, cutting patterns out, sewing armholes and necklines. Next thing we all know, it's August. Eight brand-spanking-new bridesmaid jumpsuits in plastic bags line the shop counter, each one meticulously labeled in flowery writing by Bajjo with the given name and size. Amma took one of the outfits out of its bag to have Bajjo model it for Gabina Auntie since she's the same size as one of the bridesmaids.

I can't believe we actually it pulled off, I think in awe as Bajjo parades up and down the store in the outfit while Gabina Auntie and her sister look on with unreadable expressions. Meanwhile, Gabina Auntie's niece, Uzma, the bride, is practically squealing with delight. It's been a whirlwind three weeks. *Abu will be so proud of us.*

The finished product is a work of art and it's an absolute dream on Bajjo. We used a pleated georgette fabric in a soft cornflower blue as the base with matching long jackets showcasing pearl buttons and threaded with resham—embroidery done with silver silk thread—all the way down the coat. Pink mirror needlepoint work that Amma painstakingly sewed onto each dress decorates the neckline down to the waist. The entire outfit practically flows like water. Unique. Classy. Timeless.

"They're *beautiful*!" Uzma breathes, her eyes wide and glowing. "Now I wish I'd had you design my wedding dress!"

"Maybe next time." Bajjo pretends to cough into her shoulder. Only I hear her, and I fight to contain my laugh.

Gabina Auntie seems upset that she doesn't have a reason to nitpick. Not when the bride's given us the stamp of approval. Her sister merely shrugs. "These will do. I appreciate your hard work, Naseerah."

Bajjo and I share a low five behind her back. Before I can pull back, she grabs hold of my hand and gives it a tight squeeze. It feels amazing to have my sister back, but an uncomfortable prickle climbs my throat when I remember this was the easy part. Bajjo's just reminding me that everything's going to be okay. She changes back into her own clothes and Amma folds and packs the outfit to add to the stack of others while Uzma's mom pays.

"I'm glad you like them. If you need any alterations, please feel free to bring them back for me to fix. Thank you for your business," Amma says kindly. "I do hope you'll consider working with me again in the future."

"Hmm," Gabina Auntie says tonelessly, messing with her purse's clasp. "Ambreen was right. You've certainly proven yourself. I don't mind putting in a good word for you with some of my friends."

My blood simmers. She's making it sound like we're a charity case. I'm fed up with this entitled woman and her entitled son.

"That's very kind of you," Amma replies without a hint of irritation. "I have one condition, though."

Gabina Auntie raises an eyebrow. "Condition?"

Just then, the shop doors open, and Yasir enters. Amarah and Safiya follow suit. Our strategy was for them to track him down having lunch with his crew in the town square and trick him into the store under the cover that Gabina Auntie wanted to talk to him. Knowing how he feels about his mom, I was praying he'd be too scared of her not to obey.

Yasir takes everyone in and steps back anxiously. Amarah palms him between his shoulders to hold him in place.

"What is the meaning of this?" Gabina Auntie asks. "Amarah, what do you think you're doing to your cousin?"

Yasir's eyes land on me and it's like he knows what's about to happen. He tries to escape, successfully wiggling out between Amarah and Safiya. But his path to freedom is blocked by the last person I expected to see here right now.

"You're not going anywhere," Izyaan says. Amarah and Safiya flank him on either side, effectively shutting Yasir in. He's surrounded.

"Izyaan! What do you think you're doing?" asks Gabina Auntie.

Izyaan looks from Yasir to Amarah to linger on me. He sets his jaw determinedly. "The right thing."

"Can someone please explain what's going on here?" Uzma's mom sounds very uneasy now. Uzma herself is looking around at all of us cluelessly.

Before Amma can, I speak up. "I will." All eyes train on

me. Amma, Bajjo, and Safiya give me encouraging nods. Even though sweat is already trickling on my forehead, I fill my guts with courage and say, "Yasir's been harassing me all summer. He's made inappropriate comments about my appearance and kept sending me messages even after I asked him multiple times to stop. Abdul, Shezi, and Mustafa have been in on it, too, but Yasir's the leader."

There's no time for an uncomfortable silence before Gabina Auntie is shrieking, "You little liar. My son would never do something like that."

Safiya starts to mutter under her breath, but Amarah steps in.

"She's telling the truth," Amarah says. "We all saw it for ourselves. At the masjid, of all places."

"It was obviously a misunderstanding." Gabina Auntie's voice rattles.

"No," says Izyaan. He stares his aunt down without an ounce of fear. "It wasn't. I was there when it happened more than once. I didn't say anything before, but now I am. Yasir's been treating Ainy very badly. He made fun of her when she wore the hijab." Wore. Past tense. Because I'm not wearing it today. I haven't been wearing it for almost two weeks. I was starting to get used to it, too. Taking it off was a lot harder than my decision to put it on in the first place, but in the end, Amma was the one who convinced me not to force it. Given everything that happened this summer, it just wasn't my time yet.

Amarah gives her little brother a look of approval and I finally understand who straightened Izyaan out.

"I cannot believe what I am hearing. Just because this girl likes you, Izyaan, doesn't mean you should fall for her tricks. You're accusing your own *cousin* of something very serious."

"I'm not tricking anyone!" I exclaim. "If you want proof, I have it right here." I hold up my phone. "Yasir's been contacting me through the Scope app. All of our conversations are saved."

Yasir blanches. Of course he didn't think anyone would actually read those messages, or that he would get into any real trouble.

"I've read all the messages Yasir sent Ainy," Amma inserts. "They one hundred percent fall under the category of harassment."

"He's just a kid," Gabina Auntie blubbers. I think she's more embarrassed about the fact that her sister and niece are witnessing this whole spectacle than upset about what Yasir did. "Kids make mistakes. Your daughters certainly aren't perfect. Both of them treating hijab like a game.

Putting it on and taking it off as they please. They set a horrible example."

I grind my teeth, but Amma's next words fling everyone's mouths open in surprise. "My daughters' spiritual journeys are none of your business. More importantly, they're harming no one." Amma's voice is as cold as I've ever heard it. "Unlike your son's behavior. Yasir owes Ainy an apology. Otherwise, I have no interest in working with people who insult my daughters for not doing anything wrong and instead turn a blind eye to their own child's unacceptable behavior."

Gabina Auntie throws her hands up in the air exasperatedly. "This is ridiculous! I have half a mind to have my husband march over here right now and straighten all of you out."

"Be my guest," Amma says calmly. "I've already spoken to Ambreen and her husband at length, so don't expect any support from them. I will also be contacting the other boys' parents as well, to make it clear to our community and its leaders that we will not tolerate what these boys have been doing to Ainy. Feel free to test me, Gabina."

Bright-red color mars Gabina Auntie's cheeks. Yasir cowers when she pins him with a searing gaze. He looks so young and helpless. Not like the bully who's had it out for me for weeks.

"This conversation isn't over," Gabina Auntie finally relents. "I will be speaking to my son and husband in private before taking any action. I will not have you slander my family's name."

"He's just gonna lie and act all innocent," Safiya barks, finally unable to keep it to herself. "But we know. We *know*."

"Enough," Gabina Auntie barks. "Yasir! We're leaving." Yasir doesn't even get a chance to move before Gabina Auntie yanks him away from us. Amarah smacks Yasir in the back of his head as he passes. A mortified Uzma and her mom follow them out, carrying the bridesmaid orders. None of them look back at me, Amma, Bajjo, Safiya, Amarah, or Izyaan as we're left standing inside Naseerah's Almari.

Safiya tackles me in a hug. "You were amazing."

Bajjo rubs her hands together triumphantly and high-fives Amarah. "Good riddance."

"Ainy." I turn to Izyaan and the others scatter in an effort to look busy. He scratches the side of his face, weighing his words. "I'm sorry I didn't stand up for you when the others made fun of you. Amarah lectured me after what happened at the masjid's basketball court. Told me I wasn't being neutral by staying quiet. I was taking Yasir's side and that didn't make me any better than him."

It's a bummer he hadn't thought of that before, but at least he learned his lesson. "Thanks," I say. "For standing up for me in front of your aunt. I know it must've been hard."

Izyaan shrugs, his gaze flitting this way and that. He's not sure if he should look at me, and I wonder if it's because I'm not in hijab anymore. No way I'm explaining *that* whole tale to him. He'll get used to it. Or maybe not. I don't care. I'm done with boys. Like, for the rest of my life.

Amarah and Izyaan say they'll see us at home and head out five minutes later.

"That was easy," Amma says out loud, to no one in particular. Bajjo, Safiya, and I stare at her. Then we all explode into laughter.

"I wonder what Gabina Auntie's going to do," I think out loud. Dread's curling inside my belly about how she's going to retaliate against us.

"Oh, she'll fight," Amma says. "But it won't matter because I'll fight harder. I don't care what happens to my business. My girls are the most important thing in the world to me and I would do anything to protect them."

Amma folds me and Bajjo into her arms, pressing her niqab-ed cheek to the top of my head.

"Uh, that includes me, too, right?" Safiya asks, pointing to herself dramatically.

Amma laughs and gestures Safiya forward. "Come here, you. We just delivered our biggest order yet and we're all caught up on everything else! I think we all deserve a treat. On me. Who wants ice cream?"

She doesn't have to ask us twice.

CHAPTER 26

It should not be this hard to pose for one picture with a seven-month-old baby, and yet . . .

"Noor, hold still for five seconds!" Safiya pleads. She winces as Noor shrieks joyfully and slaps her face again. "Ouch! Your nails are sharp!"

We're in the foyer of a fancy party hall, taking—*trying* to take—pictures with the photographer Safiya's parents hired for Noor's aqeeqah. Safiya didn't want two hundred people staring as she and Noor took a couple of shots together alone. Not even her parents. Only I was allowed to come watch. Surprisingly, the photo session was all Safiya's idea. Too bad it's turning out to be a disaster.

At least the photographer doesn't seem annoyed about waiting for the sisters to pull it together long enough to take a decent photo. But when they do, it's going to be the best picture ever. Both Safiya and Noor look amazing. Safiya's in a traditional Algerian karakou and Noor's dolled up in an adorable black-and-pink gharara Amma made that coordinates with the colors of Safiya's outfit. Add in the dreamlike backdrop with the humongous crystal chandelier and veined marble floors, and the Messaoudi sisters look positively royal.

"Ainy, help! Make her stop!" Safiya cries as Noor starts blowing raspberries in her face.

"Seriously, Safiya? How many times have you held her before?" I ask.

"Exactly four, including that time at the hospital when I almost dropped her on her head."

"There has to be a way to distract her," the photographer whispers to me as Safiya and Noor reengage in their power struggle. Poor Safiya really is putting her best foot forward, but Noor sure isn't making it easy. Noor's a playful baby in general, but something about being near Safiya is making her extra lively. It's like she's unleashing months of pent-up excitement all in one go. Already, I can see bits and pieces of Safiya's outgoing personality in her.

I look past the archway leading into the main party hall, where all the guests are forming two lines at the buffet table. Suha Auntie and Islam Uncle are fluttering about, making sure things run smoothly. At our long-overdue sleepover a few days ago, Safiya finally told her parents about how she's been coping with everything since Noor's birth. Suha Auntie and Islam Uncle have been working hard to make it up to her ever since. Gaining that sense of security back at home has done wonders for Safiya's self-esteem. There's no way I'm letting Safiya go back to the party feeling like a failure. Not when she's finally stepping into her big sister shoes, albeit a little clumsily.

Being a big sister is hard. I understand that even more now with everything that's happened between me and Bajjo this summer. If there's one thing I learned, my sister isn't the perfect role model that I always thought she was, but she still tries to be there for me. Sisters don't give up on each other. They love each other despite their flaws.

That's what Noor needs. For Safiya to reciprocate that love.

"Saf, stop shouting at her and ask nicely," I say.

"Ask *nicely*?" Safiya peers around Noor at me exasperatedly. "Like she's going to understand?"

"Not your words. The tone of your voice. Trust me," I insist at her dubious expression. "She just wants you to *see* her."

I hope she understands what I'm trying to say. Safiya sighs heavily and uses her knee to bounce Noor back up into her grip. Some of the tautness in her face melts away as she says something to Noor in calm Arabic. It takes Noor fifteen seconds to register the shift. She stops squirming and looks straight into Safiya's eyes. For a minute, the world stops. Everything fades into the background as Noor considers the smooth words coming out of Safiya's mouth. And that's when Noor's slobbery mouth cracks into the world's biggest grin.

"Quick, do it now!" I urge the photographer, but she was ready. In a blink, the camera flashes.

"Would you look at that," the photographer says. She leans over to share the hard-earned photo with me. I gasp at the screen. That's no ordinary picture. That's an official portrait! I can't decide what I love most about it: Noor's exuberant grin paired with her unruly curls pulled into two pigtails on top of her head or the way she's cradling Safiya's face in her tiny little hands, looking at her big sister like she's the center of her whole universe. The picture captured Safiya's expression the exact moment Noor smiled at her dotingly. Her eyes are slightly widened, her mouth parted in awe.

I run in place, waving Safiya over. "Come look at this!"

Safiya carries Noor over and her eyebrows shoot up to her hijab. "Holy crap, I'm making my parents put that front and center on top of the fireplace." Safiya grins at Noor. "What do you think?"

Noor gurgles her approval through her fist in her mouth.

"You're not so bad after all," Safiya says. "Ainy, come on! Let's take one of all three of us!"

There's my friend, I think as Safiya takes my hand in her free one and spins me in a circle. The green and maroon of my dress fan out all around me, scattering gold specks of light across the white marble floor. Noor seems to finally get the memo, because she lets us take almost a dozen shots. The photographer calls out different poses to us. Some are poised. Some downright silly. In the middle of one that involves us putting our heads together, Safiya presses her cheek to mine. I feel rather than hear her mouth *thank you*.

I put my arm around her shoulder and hug her closer. "What are sisters for?"

———◦•◦———

"Abu, are you paying attention?"

"Haan, beta. Very pretty. Did you make it? Mash Allah, is this the start of the Ainy Zain Collection?!"

I roll my eyes teasingly. "No, this one's Amma's. I was just asking for your opinion."

Abu called as soon as we got home after the aqeeqah. Even though I'm wiped out and suffering from a food coma, I dropped everything to show him the projects I'm working on in my room. Small orders that Amma's letting me take the lead on. Ever since we finished the bridesmaid jumpsuits, business has been booming. Bajjo even quit her job at Aroma to come back to Naseerah's Almari full-time. Turns out I was worried about Gabina Auntie getting revenge on us for nothing. Not with the Khalids staunchly taking our side. In the end, Yasir was given strict instructions to stay away from me. I got a handwritten apology note, which I read exactly one time before stuffing it into the bottom of my drawer. And after Sister Ambreen had a conversation with our imam, Yasir, Shezi, Abdul, and Mustafa now have to attend weekly counseling sessions.

Best of all, we got the news that my dadi's health is improving. She's not cancer-free, but the treatment is working. Abu could be back home with us in as soon as a month if she remains in stable condition.

Bajjo joins me in our room after I hang up with Abu, complaining about the mess on my side as usual. Still, she sifts through the clothes on my bed with a whole lot of interest. "Wow, this is nice." Bajjo picks up a black-and-red blouse I'm in the middle of altering for Amma's client. It's been tricky because of how delicate it is. All fabrics aren't created equal. But it's a fun challenge. There's a big difference in the quality of my work ever since Amma started giving me real-time lessons again.

"So," Bajjo muses, "are you excited?"

"About what?" I ask.

"School starts soon. You're going to seventh grade!"

"Please don't remind me." I sigh. I am not excited. Going back to school means homework, tests, and projects instead of spending time at the store. I've been having the best time designing. I don't want to stop. Amma's already said if I keep up my grades, she might change her mind and let me work at the store during the school year. But I already know I'm going to spend a lot of time waiting for *next* summer to start. Not to mention, my wardrobe is a tragedy. Bajjo misinterprets the nervous look on my face for something else.

"Yasir's not going to bother you anymore, Ainy," Bajjo assures me gently.

"It's not that. I still haven't done any shopping," I moan.

"I'll take you tomorrow," Bajjo offers. "Safiya can come, too."

I think about it. "Can it just be the two of us?" Even though all's well between Bajjo and me again, we still haven't been spending quality time together. Now that I know what life's like without Bajjo in it, I never want to feel that lost from my sister again.

Bajjo smiles. "I'd like that. Can I ask you something?"

There's nothing in her voice that should put me on guard, but I'm wary anyway. "Yeah?"

"I know we haven't really talked about it ever since that night, but have you decided if you want to be a full-time hijabi? You always said seventh grade was your year."

I pick at a loose thread on one of the dresses littering my bed. "What do you think?"

"It doesn't matter what I think," Bajjo says. She pauses. "Though I should let you know that I'm going to start wearing mine again."

My head snaps in her direction. "You are?"

Bajjo pulls her legs up and hugs them to her chest. "Yep. I thought about it a lot. Made lots of dua. And I realized I don't care what anybody says anymore. If I want to be the best at something, it'll be because I want to be, not because of the pressures put on me. I shouldn't have let people get to me. I'm allowed to be human and make mistakes. I mean, come on. I'm sixteen. I'm allowed to be a messy teenager. As long as Allah knows that I'm trying my best, it's worth it. It's worth being myself. It's not a straight road. I have to renew my intentions constantly. Remind myself why I wear it. *Who* I'm wearing it for. It's not for Amma or Abu, or boys, or my friends, or you. I do it for myself. For Him. And I'm happier wearing it than I am without it."

I grin. "I'm sorry I expected so much of you. You'll always be good enough for me, no matter what." I wanted Amma and Bajjo to be superhuman so that I could feed off their strength, when in reality, I needed to build up my own. "But . . . I don't know if I'm ready." I hate to admit it, but there are still voices inside my head that are influencing me. Telling me that I'm not worthy, and that no one's going to take my modest fashion design dreams seriously, which I know isn't true. I want wearing the hijab to be about me and my faith, not about anyone or anything else. The only person I need to prove anything to is myself, and I'm the only person who can demand that others respect me. Not the presence of my hijab. I know I have it in me to commit to the hijab at some point. Just not right now. I still have so much to learn.

About designing clothes. About my deen. About myself. I'll get there.

"When you are," Bajjo says, "I promise I've got your back this time. We face enough opposition as it is. I'm the last person you should feel worried about. I was just trying to protect you."

My heart puffs with glee. "Thanks, Bajjo."

"Hey, you guys." Kashif glares at us from the doorway with a box of Clorox wipes in his hand. "Amma's asking why the floor looks like it hasn't been cleaned in days?"

Bajjo blows a strand of her hair out of her face in annoyance. "That's Ainy's job."

"I've been busy!" I protest. Kashif throws the Clorox at me and I dodge it with a yelp.

"Right now?" I grumble. "I haven't even changed yet!"

"Better get on that before Amma gets on your case," Bajjo says, lying back with her hands behind her head.

"Some siblings," I mumble, and procrastinate by sorting out the mess on my side. I'm putting away a box of buttons in my nightstand when I see the corner of a teal-green scarf poking out. My first-day hijab. I rub the soft cloth between my fingers sadly. I guess I should put it somewhere else now. Carefully, I fold the scarf in my lap, then move to put it on the top shelf of my cluttered closet.

It's not a *goodbye*. It's a *see you later. One day.*

One day when I'm ready, I'll put the hijab on proudly and never look back. And I'll do it for You. I promise. The silent prayer leaves my heart and I clutch my hand to my chest like I'm trying to secure the words into an invisible locket, to wear and carry around with me until my dua finally comes true.

Until then, I'm going to keep designing, and showing the world that modest is beautiful, too.

AUTHOR'S NOTE

I have seen and heard many concerning stories from women and girls in my life—Muslim and non-Muslim— about behaviors and comments they are subjected to that are too often swept under the rug or chalked up to "boys will be boys." Then in 2020, I read Barbara Dee's *Maybe He Just Likes You*. It was the first book I read that addressed the issue of sexual harassment for young kids and it made me realize that this theme can be in a book for young readers.

At the same time, global conversations surrounding hijab—whether to enforce or to ban—were frustrating to me. It seemed like everyone's opinion on the matter was being asked for except for the opinion of Muslim women who simply want their freedom. No one should have their bodily autonomy taken away from them.

Ainy's story was born from these two ideas coming together: a story about a girl who must find a way to stand up for herself when she starts getting unwanted attention from a boy who doesn't know when to quit, as well as my attempt to remind people that hijab is part of a very personal spiritual journey. As Kulsoom says, there will always be people who will have an opinion of you. They will tell you that you're not good enough. But my hope is that you can figure out your own truth and set yourself on a path that feels right for you.

Though this is a work of fiction, many of the uncomfortable situations, conversations, and comments Ainy is subjected to throughout the book are either drawn from my own personal experience or the experiences of people I know. Additionally, Ainy's journey with hijab as depicted in this book is just one example of a young Muslim girl taking a conscious step toward her Creator. The decision to start observing hijab can happen at any stage in life. I always intended *Any Way You Look* to be about a character at the very beginning of this emotional journey.

It should also go without saying that Yasir and his friends do not portray or represent all Muslim boys and men. I'm proud to have male figures in my life who embody strong morals as demonstrated by the Prophet (PBUH) and who love and respect the rights of all people. Extra gratitude to all those in our community who have zero tolerance for sexual harassment—the ones who are not afraid to call out this very serious issue and work tirelessly to educate the next generation.

To my readers: If you or someone you know finds yourselves in a similar situation to Ainy's, please do not shy away from speaking up. I know that asking for help is hard, even from those we trust, but your voice can make all the difference.

GLOSSARY

almari—the Urdu word for a physical wardrobe or closet

awrah—the intimate parts of the human body, according to Islam, that must be covered by clothing

dawat—the Urdu word for a formal get-together to celebrate any joyous occasion

deen—the Arabic word for the religion or belief of a Muslim

dunya—the Arabic word for the temporal world and its earthly concerns and possessions

sadaqah—the Arabic word for voluntary charity

ACKNOWLEDGMENTS

Fragments of Ainy's story had been brewing in my head for years. Then one day, my agent, Lauren Spieller, suggested I combine the character arc of one idea that I had with the plot of another, and the result is the book you now hold in your hands. It's only fitting that Lauren be the first one that I express my gratitude to. So, thank you, Lauren! Without your advice, who knows how long Ainy's story would've had to wait for its turn to be told?

To my editor, Emily Seife: This is our third book together and I think it's our best collaboration to date. Thank you for believing in me and Ainy. But most of all, thank you for being so enthusiastic about the stories I want to tell and for always pushing me to give them my best effort. Sorry about the Almond Joy diss!

I'm so grateful to Kassy Lopez, Janell Harris, Jessica White, Priscilla Eakeley, Esther Reisberg, and Richard Gonzalez, Jr. for all the hard work they put into turning *Any Way You Look* into a real book. To Rachel Feld and Katie Dutton in marketing, Emily Heddleson and Lizette

Serrano in library marketing, Aleah Gornbein and Seale Ballenger in publicity, David Levithan, Ellie Berger, and the entire sales team—thank you for all that you do to spread the joy of reading and for making Scholastic such a wonderful home for my books.

Thank you times a hundred to illustrator Sara Alfageeh, designer Omou Barry, and art director Elizabeth Parisi for the absolutely stunning cover. You all knocked it out of the park. I still can't believe how perfect it is.

All my love to Lauren Blackwood and Laura Weymouth for keeping me sane with their advice and support through life's ups and downs. I live for our chats and video calls!

Thank you to my whole family for proudly sharing my books with people outside our family. I'm not cool by any stretch of the imagination, but y'all sure make me feel like I am sometimes. Special shout-out to Islam (the man, not the religion) for answering all my questions about Algerian culture and for allowing me to give you and Suha a fictional daughter!

To my parents and parents-in-law, whom I will never be able to repay for the opportunities they give me to chase my dreams.

To my husband, Usman, my forever number one

supporter. I have no words for how much I love and appreciate you.

To my local independent bookstore, Scrawl Books, for your continued enthusiasm for my books and for being a warm light in our community.

To my readers, for the love and support you have given me and my books. Thank you for picking them up. Whenever I feel down about my writing is the exact moment when one of you will reach out with a kind email that immediately gives me the boost I need to keep going.

And lastly, as always, thank you, Allah (SWT), for helping me find my words and for hearing even the smallest of prayers.

ABOUT THE AUTHOR

MALEEHA SIDDIQUI is an American writer of Pakistani descent who loves to tell stories for all ages about the American Muslim experience. She can't live without caffeine, rainy days, and books with a whole lot of heart. Her previous novels, *Barakah Beats* and *Bhai for Now*, were both Junior Library Guild Gold Standard Selections. *Barakah Beats* was also an ABA Indies Introduce pick. By day, Maleeha works in the biotech industry. She grew up and continues to reside with her family in Virginia. Find her at maleehasiddiqui.com and on Instagram at @malsidink.